THE APOSTATE

and Other Tales of the Southwest

also by

J.B. HOGAN

Tin Hollow

Time & Time Again

Fallen: A Short Story Collection

Bar Harbor: A Short Story Collection

The Rubicon: A Poetry Collection

Losing Cotton

Living Behind Time

Nonfiction

Angels in the Ozarks

Forgotten Fayetteville & Washington County

THE APOSTATE

and Other Tales of the Southwest

J.B. HOGAN

An imprint of Roan & Weatherford Publishing Associates, LLC
Bentonville, Arkansas
www.roanweatherford.com

Library of Congress Cataloging-in-Publication Data
Names: Hogan, J.B., author.
Title: The Apostate and Other Tales of the Southwest/J.B. Hogan |
Description: Second Edition | Bentonville: Rogue River, 2024.
Identifiers: ISBN: 978-1-63373-941-3 (paperback) | ISBN: 978-1-63373-942-0 (eBook)
Subjects: BISAC: FICTION/Crime | FICTION/Short Stories (single author)
FICTION/General

Rogue River trade paperback edition May, 2024

Cover & Interior Design by Casey W. Cowan
Editing by Amy Cowan

Table of Contents

THE APOSTATE

1

MICHAEL WRIGHT FELT cold metal against his left temple and closed his eyes. It was a .38 he guessed. A Saturday Night Special. The only kind the frantic boy beside him probably could afford or get his hands on. Irrational anger at his wife pulsed through Michael's shocked system. The stupid ring could have been picked up any time. But Barbara had to have him go get it right then. And it wasn't even ready.

Very briefly, he considered jumping the boy—smelly and ragged as the kid was in his filthy jeans and threadbare, once-black Anthrax T-shirt—but the boy suddenly tensed up, and Michael let that idea go as quickly as it had popped into his head.

Anthrax? What the hell was Anthrax. Some kind of band? A heavy metal band? Of course. Carjacked by a head banger boy and his poor white trash girlfriend up front driving. How could this have happened? How was it possible? He figured he must have snapped, gone over the edge without realizing it. Or maybe it was an acid flashback. But when he looked out the window, barely moving his head so that the boy wouldn't go nuts and shoot him, he saw the swap meet go by, and he knew he was really where he was. Kidnapped. Carjacked. Racing out of Tucson, presumably toward the interstate. To where? Old Mexico? New Mexico? Phoenix? God only knew.

This is karma, Michael thought bitterly. Karma. Cause and effect.

This was the effect from a cause he had caused. Some time, somewhere. And the hammer had come down across the years. He knew he deserved this. He didn't want it anyway.

"Karma." He closed his eyes again.

"What?" The boy jammed the pistol harder into Michael's temple.

"Nothing. Nothing."

"What did he say, Bobby Earl?" The girl driving called back over her right shoulder.

"Nothin'."—Bobby Earl pointed at her to pay attention to the road—"he's just mumblin' crap."

"Don't you hurt him, now. You promised."

"He keeps his mouth shut, I won't." Bobby Earl ground the .38 barrel into Michael's head.

"Take it easy." Michael dared to say.

"Shut up."

"There's an overpass comin' up, Bobby, which way do I go? Do I take the interstate?"

"How the hell do I know, Mary Beth? You gotta make some decisions on your own. I'm watchin' this dumb ass. Or I can shoot him and come up there and drive my ownself. Is that what you want me to do?"

"Don't you shoot him, Bobby Earl. Don't you do that."

"Then shut up and get us on the stupid interstate."

"I don't know which exit to take." Mary Beth's voice quivered. "Which is it? Which way? El Paso or Phoenix? East or west?"

"Go west to El Paso."

"El Paso's east." Michael was unable to resist a teacher's urge to correct an error.

"What did he say?"

"Don't know. But he better shut his ugly piehole is all I got to say."

"El Paso is east," Michael repeated softly, unwisely.

"You dumb shit." Bobby Earl laughed. "Lights out."

"IT DOESN'T MATTER." Barbara acted like it was of little concern, but Michael knew it most assuredly mattered. "I'll go myself later. If you're too busy."

"No, no." Michael downed his seventh and eighth Tylenols of the day with a swallow of nauseatingly warm tap water. Central Arizona Project water, he thought, lucky it wasn't brown and smelly. He massaged the bridge of his nose behind his heavy, plastic lens glasses. His head hurt all the time anymore. "I'll go. Do you want me to go now?"

"You don't have to go right now." Michael knew better.

If fifteen years of marriage had taught him anything about his wife, it was that when she locked onto a task she wanted done, that task was to be taken care of immediately. She would continue to discuss that lack of importance and that there was no hurry in getting it done until Michael got up and did it. Simple as that.

He figured it was some kind of misdirected energy related to their childless and, after all these years, passionless union. And he couldn't blame her for the way she felt. After all, he had saddled her with a life of boring mediocrity and had steadfastly refused to play the father to the mother role she had increasingly desired over the years, but he resented it anyway.

"Where is this store?" He rubbed his neck and twisted it from side to side.

"It's in El Con. You remember. Next to the health food store. But you don't have to go now."

"I'm going." Michael's head hurt worse than before, and when he closed his eyes, everything was red and burning.

"You don't need to."

"I'm leaving. Which car should I take?"

"Take the Accord. Your car is almost out of gas. And pick up some more Christmas paper, will you? I need to wrap the dean's gift if we're going to his Godawful party tomorrow night."

"Okay." Michael headed out the front door.

He let the door slam shut over some last directions and hurried out to the Accord. At least it was nice and cool for a change. He started the engine and pressed the button to automatically lower the driver's side window. The heat had lasted so far into the fall, he felt like some internal thermostat had snapped and he would never be able to stand another Tucson summer. He craved cool air now like a fish craved water. Sucking air through his nose, he felt a lessening of the continual head pain.

By the time he got to El Con, avoiding the usual three to four attempts of fellow Tucsonans to kill or maim him with their automobiles, he was feeling halfway normal. He found a space in the crowded lot south of the main entrance to the mall and parked the Accord.

Damn, he complained silently, climbing out of the vehicle, did I forget the money? Speaking to himself, either in his own head or sometimes, embarrassingly, out loud, was a habit that had increased over the last few deathly uninspiring years. Once a promising young academic, Michael's career in the University of Arizona English department had stalled at the Associate Professor level. He had been put on the back burner, both in terms of his career and the courses he taught, as the new young lions and lionesses bypassed him in position and tenure.

He closed the door of the Honda and checked his billfold. There was a hell of a lot of money in there, he realized with surprise, becoming aware that it was not too smart to flash big wads of cash like that anywhere in Tucson anymore. It wasn't L.A. by any stretch of the imagination, but Tucson wasn't the sleepy little stucco burg it had been years before either. Re-pocketing the billfold, he nearly ran into a young woman standing by the back fender of an old junker Chevy parked in the slot next to his.

"Oh, I'm sorry." He staggered to his left to avoid bumping into the girl. She held out a hand to steady him.

"It's okay, mister." She apologized. Michael focused on her, stared into a pair of the saddest, sweetest eyes he'd seen in years.

"Thank you." The girl's hand slipped from his arm. "I'm just getting clumsy anymore."

"That's all right." Michael heard for the first time a distinct southern accent.

He also noticed the girl was good looking in a plain, non-traditional way and that her light, cotton print dress revealed a lean, lanky body—raw-boned was the old term—highlighted by pronounced breasts and wide hips. A child-bearing body. The phrase "barefoot and pregnant" popped into his head. The girl had long, stringy brown hair, and her face was very white, but she had kind, green eyes, a thin nose, and lips not quite full enough to make her pretty by conventional standards. Michael liked her immediately.

"Pardon me."

As he passed the back of the girl's vehicle on the way to the mall entrance, a young man got out of the driver's seat. Michael glanced at him long enough to get a vague impression—skinny, long dirty hair, dark clothing, some kind of testosterone-based smirk of disrespect. Michael averted his eyes and hustled on to the store.

Inside, the mall was so busy it could have served as a human version of an ant farm. People bustled in every direction, laughing, shouting, hurrying from one shop to the next in a frenzy of consumer activity. Michael reeled from the movement and sound. He hated malls. Hated the mindless consumerism they represented to him. Hated the sights and smells, the noise, of so much humanity in such close quarters doing nothing but spending their hard-earned dollars on useless throwaway items.

Resting for a moment against the window of an antiseptically clean-smelling clothing store, he braced himself and then plunged through the crowd into what he hoped was the right jewelry store. A young sales clerk spoke to him from across the ring and necklace-filled glass counter.

"May I help you, sir?" Her friendly voice penetrated Michael's foggy consciousness. He smiled at her. She waited for him to speak.

"Oh… oh." He fumbled in his billfold for the ticket Barbara had given him. "I wanted to see if our ring is ready yet." He reached the ticket over to the girl.

"I'll be just a moment."

Michael watched the girl walk to the back of the store. She was blonde and thin. Her pretty face was too made up, and she was somehow out of place in the jewelry store. A recent high school grad, he figured, somebody's darling daughter, treading water before college or marriage to some boy next door type. Eighteen, he guessed, squeaky clean, perfectly normal, achingly cute to a worn out, middle-aged man. He wondered if he had properly appreciated young women her age when he had been young himself. He seriously doubted it. He knew he hadn't.

"I'm sorry, sir." The girl returned with the ticket. "It's not back yet. Maybe you can try again later? This time of year we're so busy, we might not get another delivery from our adjustment person until evening."

"Evening?" Michael wondered what an "adjustment person" was. "Uh, when do you close?"

"Eight o'clock, sir."

"Okay, thanks. I'll try back later."

"Thank you, sir. Have a good day."

Michael put the ticket back in his billfold and re-entered the fair-like atmosphere of the mall corridors. He had really disliked it from the very first time a young woman had called him sir. What a drag it was to get old, he thought. What a drag indeed. Then, lowering his head as if steeling himself for a blast of cold Midwest winter wind, he headed for the exit.

He still had to pick up some Christmas paper. But he'd go to a smaller store for that. Some little mom and pop place. More expensive but with a better atmosphere to it. A feeling of hominess and safety. With a marginally renewed sense of satisfaction, he walked out of the mall's main south exit and headed back to the car.

MICHAEL OPENED HIS right eye first. Slowly, painfully. Then the left eye. He hadn't been out long. He saw the exit sign for Sixth Avenue go by. From the high pitch in her voice, the girl driving was losing it. The boy beside him was doing his usual cursing.

"Goddamn it, Mary Beth, you got us goin' the wrong way."

"The signs say Nogales one way or Phoenix the other," Mary Beth wailed, "what do I do? Where do I go?"

"You dumbass, we're supposed to be going to El Paso, what are you doin'?"

"Stop yelling at me, Bobby Earl, stop cursing me. I don't know where we're at. I don't know where El Paso is."

"Don't hit me." Michael sat up slowly. "Take it easy." Bobby Earl held the .38 threateningly above Michael's head. "El Paso is behind us. If you go to the right up here, toward Phoenix, you can get off at the first exit and then cross under the interstate and head back east."

"Why would we go east to El Paso?" Bobby Earl wanted to know. "It's out west."

"The west Texas town of El Paso." Mary Beth peered into the rear-view mirror.

"But it's east of here," Michael explained. "We're farther west than El Paso."

"You better not be screwin' around." Bobby Earl growled.

"You got the gun." Michael held up his hands. "It wouldn't make any sense to screw around."

"Yeah," Bobby Earl allowed.

"Here, mister?" Mary Beth crossed into the exit lane.

"Yes. Take this one."

"You mess around with us," Bobby Earl threatened, "I'll blow your rich butt away."

"Rich?" Michael instinctively reached back to check for his bill-fold. It was gone. Naturally.

"Lookin' for this?" Bobby Earl laughed, holding up the missing billfold. It looked completely empty to Michael. So much for the four hundred he'd had.

"Now I cross under and go back to the left?" Mary Beth glanced back at Michael.

"Yes." He took the billfold from Bobby Earl. It was empty, except for a couple of pictures—one of Barbara's baby nephew, another of Michael and Barbara from an earlier, not so deadened time.

"It says El Paso to the left," Mary Beth called out happily.

"Whad'ya know, rich boy." Bobby Earl waggled the pistol. "You got lucky."

"I'm a lucky kind of guy."

"Shut up, piss ant."

"Yes." Michael agreed. "I will."

2

PRODDED BY BOBBY Earl's frequent, if erratic, outbursts, Mary Beth nervously guided the Honda east on I-10. They passed the big IBM plant, then Vail, and on toward Benson. Out of the corner of his eye, Michael saw a huge, castle-like house sitting high on a hill north of the interstate and wished he were there—there or anywhere but in his carjacked vehicle heading to El Paso. As they sped around a long, slow curve in the highway approaching Benson proper, Bobby Earl suddenly became more agitated than he already was, more paranoid. He apparently sensed some kind of trouble.

"Take that exit there," he yelled at Mary Beth, shifting his body away from Michael and up onto the edge of the back seat.

"Right here?"

"Do it. Get off the interstate."

Mary Beth slowed the Honda and drove down into Benson. Bobby Earl had her pull over at the side of a fruit stand. The same stand, Michael noted ironically to himself, that he and Barbara had stopped at years ago on their way to Tombstone. It was their first excursion after moving to Tucson, and they had been happy and affectionate then. It was light years and another galaxy away from the present.

"What are we doing, Bobby Earl?" Mary Beth turned toward the back seat. She surprised Michael with something like a reassuring smile.

"Just wait a minute. Take it easy."

"I don't see…."

"Shh." Bobby Earl put his left index finger to his lips.

Michael cocked his head at a distant sound. His heart raced, and his breath came rapidly, shallow. The whine of a police siren, coming from the west, from Tucson, became clear, grew louder, split the air as the vehicle raced by on the interstate, lights flashing. His heart sank as it whipped by, hope dying with the diminishing sound. Bobby Earl jumped around beside him, laughing wildly, hitting the back of the front seat with his free hand.

"How did you know he was comin'? How did you know?"

"I'm Clyde Barrow, baby." Bobby Earl boasted. "I'm Pretty Boy Floyd. I'm John Dillinger."

"They all got caught. They all got killed." Michael immediately cringed at his own foolish, big mouth.

"You are a stupid asshole." Bobby Earl pressed the .38 hard against Michael's jaw and pulled the hammer back. Michael froze, stopped breathing.

"Bobby Earl!" Mary Beth cried.

"What do we need this idiot for, anyway?" The boy countered. "I'll show him who got killed."

"You promised. You're not to hurt him or anyone. Let's just let him go."

Michael tried to express his gratitude to the girl with his eyes—and without moving a muscle. She didn't look at him.

"He's just in the way," Bobby Earl groused. "Nobody would notice he was gone anyway. He's nothin' but a loser. An old yuppie."

"You don't hurt him."

"Then he's a hostage. If we get in trouble, we swap him. If anybody would want the useless son of a bitch. What do you do anyway, rich boy?"

"I… I'm a professor."

"A professor? He's a professor. Whoop de fuckin' do. Whad'ya say, Prof, I waste you or take you along?"

"Bobby." Mary Beth tilted her head and tightened her mouth like she was correcting a bad child.

"All right." The boy uncocked the .38 and pulled it away from Michael's face. "You're safe for now, Prof. You're lucky she's here to protect you."

"I know," Michael whispered. "I know."

"Let's go, Mary Beth."

"Which way now?"

"Back out to the interstate. To El Paso."

"There's a back way out of here to the interstate," Michael offered carefully.

"Really, mister?"

"Yes."

"You better not be messin' around."

"I'm not."

3

MICHAEL DIRECTED HIS captors through Benson and out the east side of the little town, across an old metal bridge, and then back onto the interstate. Except for the boy's crowing that he had another escape route from the cops now that Michael's tip had been on the level, the group rode pretty much in silence toward Texas Canyon. But when the billboard signs for "The Thing" started showing up, Bobby Earl reanimated.

"The Thing? What the hell's The *Thing?* Is that some kind of, uh, weird alien or something?"

"I don't know." Mary Beth didn't look over. "Maybe he knows."

"What about it, Prof?" Bobby Earl moved the .38 barrel back and forth in front of Michael's face. "What is that? Is it on the level? What is it, some kind of space monster or something like that?"

"Something like that." Despite being scared witless by the gun-wagging boy, Michael couldn't restrain his natural bent toward sarcasm.

"You know,"—Bobby Earl frowned—"I'm pretty sick of you already, teacher boy."

"Sorry. I've never seen The Thing. Somebody I knew once stopped there, and it was like some phony mummy deal or something. A waste of money."

"Yeah, well, maybe to you highbrow uppity types it probably is.

I'd kinda like to check it out myself. What do you say, Mary Beth? Want to stop?"

"Lord, no, Bobby. We'd get picked up for sure if we just stopped."

"Yeah, but I wanted to see it. Crap." They passed the ad-tattooed building housing "The Thing" a few minutes later. "I'd a liked to seen that."

"We will some other time, hon." Mary Beth reassured him.

Michael controlled an urge to let out a big sigh or a judgmental shaking of the head. He didn't know what he expected—to be car-jacked by a couple of honor students? What a screwed up situation he was in and all because he wasn't paying attention in the El Con Mall parking lot. Well, he was paying the price now.

For a quarter of an hour, then, they drove on in silence. Mary Beth concentrated on the road ahead, Bobby Earl twirled the .38 around in his right hand, Michael sulked—blaming his fate on Barbara, on the God he didn't believe in, and finally back where it belonged, back to himself. Looking out the window forlornly, he had just seen a sign for Willcox when Bobby Earl suddenly cried out.

"There, there," he yelled at Mary Beth. "Get off here. Take that dirt road off to the right. See out there? There's some kind of a big plant or something out there. See?"

"I see it."

"Slow up and get off."

Mary Beth easily made the next exit, and in moments they were rumbling along on the dirt road, a dust tail lifting up behind them as they went. With each minute they traveled away from the interstate, Michael's fear grew. And when Bobby Earl directed Mary Beth to turn off onto an even smaller—almost trail-like—road, Michael's heart pounded, and his pulse throbbed.

"What are we goin' down here for?" Mary Beth saw that the trail got narrower and narrower.

They were approaching what was apparently some kind of shallow manmade lake. Across the lake was the plant, maybe some kind of mining operation. The trail side was surrounded by tall grass, and near the edge of the lake by a stand of cattails, Bobby Earl had Mary Beth stop where he figured the car couldn't be seen.

"Leave the motor on."

"What are we gonna do?" She turned around in the seat to face Bobby Earl and Michael.

"You don't worry about it none."

"He's going to shoot me," Michael worked up the courage to say. He figured he was dead now anyway. Why hold back?

"He'll do no such thing, will you, Bobby? You promised."

"I'm thinkin' about it."

"Bobby Earl Bunton!"

"What?"

"You know very well what."

"I promised not to hurt the dumb jerk. So what? Who cares?"

"I do." Mary Beth's angry declaration echoed Michael's silent, internal response.

"What for?"

"You forget I got little Marcie Kay."

"She's with your mama in Fort Smith."

"That ain't the point."

"Well, what the hell is the point, then?"

"The point is I want to go back to my baby. I love her, Bobby Earl. More'n anything. If you let this nice gentleman go, we can just drive on and get back home. If you hurt him, the police will be after us forever."

"They'll be looking for me forever, anyway." Bobby Earl was petulant. "They's always after me. My whole life. Ever since I was a kid."

"I know they was, baby." Mary Beth reached back to run her hand gently along the side of Bobby Earl's face.

"You know they was always out to get me. 'Cause I'm a Bunton. 'Cause of my old man. Never let us alone. Daddy never done nothin' but try to get what was rightfully his."

"I know, hon."

"Cops and pissants like this dumbhead." Bobby Earl aimed the .38

at Michael. "Always acting like they're better than me. You better'n me, Professor, you stinkin' jerk?"

"No, I'm not, Bobby Earl."

"Damn straight." The boy pointed the weapon away from Michael.

"You just need some soothin's all." Mary Beth put her hand on Bobby Earl's thigh. He and Michael looked down at her hand. Mary Beth winked at Bobby Earl.

"Oh, baby, that'd be good. Where?"

"Over in them cattails?"

"What about college boy?"

"He ain't got nowhere to go. We got the keys."

"I'll be watchin' you all the time, Professor." Bobby Earl waggled the .38 at Michael again.

"Don't try to run, mister." The girl shut off the engine. "We'll let you off up in the next town or something."

"Okay." Michael tried to sound sincere. He planned to make a run for it the minute the boy and girl got into the cattails.

"Maybe we can drop him off up the road. Then park the car somewhere and catch a bus back home. Nobody'll know nothin'."

"What kind of harebrained idea is that?" Bobby Earl objected but not strongly. Mary Beth's insistent rubbing on the inside of his thighs was having its effect.

"I swear I won't say anything about either of you." Michael tried not to watch the girl stimulating Bobby Earl.

"Shut up, fool. C'mon, baby, you got me all fired up now."

The boy threatened Michael again with the .38 and then pressed the automatic door lock as he and Mary Beth climbed out of the car. They had only gotten a few yards away, nowhere near the cattails, when Bobby Earl dropped his pants, and Mary Beth knelt before him. Michael's instinct was to turn away, but he forced himself to watch Bobby Earl, waiting for a moment when the young tough would be so caught up in pleasure that Michael could unlock the door and make his break.

Finally, Michael saw Bobby Earl give himself up to his senses, his gun hand dropped to his side—head rolled back and eyes closed. With a minimum of movement, Michael reached over the front seat, pressed the automatic lock, grabbed the door handle opposite where Bobby Earl and Mary Beth had gone out and bolted from the vehicle.

He paused briefly at the back of the car, hunched down out of sight, then ran up the path as fast as he could. One shot was all it took to halt the escape. The explosive roar of the .38 and the whistling of the round ripping through the nearby tall grass by his head froze him in his tracks.

"You stupid son of a bitch." He heard the boy yell.

Michael cringed, listened to Bobby Earl's thudding footsteps approaching—pants down around his ankles Michael wondered?—and then the boy was on him, hacking him in the back of the neck with the pistol. He hit the ground with a thud, face flat into the dirt and grass along the path. Bobby Earl jerked him up with his free hand. He cocked the .38 and aimed it at Michael's head just when Mary Beth intervened again.

"Stop, Bobby, stop." She pushed the weapon to one side.

"Damn it, Mary Beth, this idiot's gonna get us caught. I'm goin' to blow him away."

"No, you're not." Mary Beth pushed herself between Michael and the boy. "Not while I'm around." She grabbed Michael and shoved him back to the car. "We'll tie him up in the car. He won't do nothin' else, will you, mister?"

"No." Michael muttered, spitting out dirt and grass. He couldn't believe this girl kept saving his life. Twice already. "I won't try anything else."

"You better not, you stupid ignorant son of a bitch bastard." Bobby Earl elevated his invective to new levels.

"Maybe there's something to tie him up with."

"How do you get in the trunk of this car?" Bobby Earl growled. Michael didn't volunteer that there was a handle by the front seat. Mary Beth handed the keys to the boy. "Well, whad'ya know." He laughed when he had unlocked and opened the trunk.

"What?"

"The dork's nice enough to have a couple of pieces of this here nylon cord for us."

Michael had used the cord to tie down the Christmas tree he and Barbara bought the week before. He had tossed the cord in the trunk because he was simply too lazy to store it in the garage.

"Thanks, stupid college professor." Bobby Earl laughed.

Mary Beth held the .38 while the boy tied up Michael's hands and then his ankles—both very tightly and painfully.

"Okay." Bobby Earl nodded when he was done. "Help me put him back in the car, and let's get out of here. Somebody might have heard that shot."

4

"YOU HAVE A couple of hot reports, Boss." Carol Norris informed Dave Bishop as he came in out of the bright but cool Albuquerque afternoon. "Ralph has them back in the office."

"Good stuff?" Dave winked at his efficient secretary.

Carol had been with him since the beginning five years ago. Dave had quit his job as a detective on the Albuquerque police force and opened up his own private investigation business. It had been slow going at first, then picked up enough to hire Ralph Ortega—an ex-cop from Socorro—to help Dave find the usual not-really-missing persons and the definitely cheating husbands and wives.

In the last year, Dave and Ralph had begun taking on occasional bounty hunter work—bail jumpers, deadbeat alimony dads, that sort of thing—and now they had more work than they could sometimes handle. Carol had been through all that with Dave, and now Ralph, and she was indispensable.

"Ralph's got the specifics." Carol credited her other boss. "But I think one of them is about that kid from Arkansas. You know, the one who jumped bail in Oklahoma and maybe hit that convenience store in Santa Rosa."

"Oh, yeah. What was it, Bindley or Burton?"

"Bunton, I believe, Boss."

"Right, Bunton. Nasty little boy."

"Sounds like it."

"Okay, I'll check it out, see what Ralphie's got."

"Your mom called, too," Carol added as Dave started toward the door of his and Ralph's office. "Something about Christmas shopping."

"Oh, crap, almost forgot. I promised to take her shopping for presents tonight. Thanks, Carol. I wouldn't know what to do without you."

"You're welcome, Mister Bishop." Dave winked at her again and went into his office.

"What's up, Partner?"

Stocky Ralph Ortega sat at the big desk the two men shared. One or the other of them was usually out of the office, so they had decided to use the same office and desk to save on expenses.

"They found our boy's car in Tucson." Ralph didn't look up from several printouts he had spread across the desk.

Dave could see the balding crown on the dark-haired, ex-marine, ex-middleweight fighter's head. Ralph was a good partner. Solid, straight, dependable. Very little nonsense. Maybe a little weak in the sense of humor department. But Dave had known a lot of cops and ex-cops like that himself. The lack of such was one of the reasons—among dozens—that his ex-wife had given for leaving him some years back. That and his penchant for all night work—or drink-a-thons as she called them. But he couldn't very well blame her for that—she was right.

"Let me guess." Dave held up his right hand to stop Ralph from giving any more details. "It was some kind of junker, probably a Chevy or Ford, Oklahoma plates—expired—and the subject, read perp, has managed to evade local law enforcement. How'm I doin'?"

"Darned good." Ralph gave Dave a thin smile. "You left out the Santa Rosa clerk's description of our boy wonder and that she remembered three numbers off the Oklahoma plates."

"Definitely our boy, then?"

"Right. Bobby Earl Bunton. White male, born in Alma, Arkansas. His sheet includes breaking and entering—"

"Yeah, I know all that."

"Check out this other report."

"What's it about?"

"Same time as the Tucson police report finding the perp's vehicle, there was a carjacking."

"Stolen vehicles and carjacking?" Dave laughed without humor. "Who'd have thought? There were probably two or three more the same day. They learn it in L.A., take it to Tucson"

"Tucson's not nearly that bad," Ralph objected. "It's a nice town. Not as good as before but still nice."

"Yeah, you're probably right."

"Just listen to this, Dave. This is the intriguing part."

"Go on."

"Two things—one, the Bunton vehicle and the carjacking were at the same mall over there. The, uh, El Con Mall."

"Okay." Dave's interest perked up.

"And two, witness accounts match pretty closely the Santa Rosa clerk's description of our perp. Also, just like in Santa Rosa, there was somebody with Bunton, possibly a woman."

"Getting good." Dave digested the information. "What do we have on the victim or victims?"

"A college professor, apparently, at least there's one who went missing about the same time. Silver Honda four door, Arizona plate VGH 327."

"Got a name?"

"Yeah, says here Michael Wright. Been at the University for several years now, he's a…."

"Michael Wright? Michael Wright. That sounds really—"

A knock on the office door popped Dave out of his thoughts. Carol came in with another report. She gave it to Dave. He read it and handed it to Ralph.

"I'm going down there," Dave stated.

"I'll come with you."

"No, Ralphie boy, stay here. Man the info. I'll keep in touch from the car. I got a feeling on this one."

"Uh-oh, a feeling? You becoming a touchy-feely PI?" Dave laughed.

"What about your mother?" Carol reminded Dave.

"Would you be a sweetheart, Carol? Could you take her out for me?"

"Well, sure, I guess."

"I'll be back as soon as I can." Dave headed for the door. "Ralphie, see if you can get a photo of the victim. You can send it to me somewhere along the road."

"Socorro," Ralph called out to the retreating figure of his partner. "I'll send it to my buds in Socorro."

The door slammed shut, leaving Carol staring at Ralph in disbelief. "Goodness, did you get the name of the typhoon that just blew out of here?"

"You know, Dave. When he gets a hunch...."

"He always follows up." Carol completed the sentence.

"Always." Ralph smiled his thin smile.

5

BOBBY EARL HAD them pull off in Willcox and go through a fast food drive-thru. He had Mary Beth order two double cheeseburgers, fries, and an Orange Slice for him, a hamburger, fries, and Mountain Dew for her.

"What would you like, mister?" Mary Beth turned toward Michael.

"To hell with him."

"He's gotta eat something, Bobby Earl. What'll it be, mister, a hamburger, cheeseburger?'

"I'm a vegetarian." Michael deigned to say.

"What?" Bobby Earl exploded.

"I don't eat meat."

"I know what a vegetarian is, you butthole. A vegetarian? How stupid is that?"

"You have to respect everyone's right to their own way of eatin', Bobby Earl." Mary Beth allowed.

"Could I have a fish sandwich?" Michael took in Mary Beth's plain, pretty face and benevolent smile. How in the world, he wondered, did she get hooked up with this crazy boy?

"Fish?" Bobby Earl laughed. "Fish? You ain't no vegetarian. What the hell is that?"

"I don't eat meat."

"The hell you don't. What exactly kind of vegetable is a fish, huh, Mister College Professor?"

"Oh, hush, Bobby Earl." Mary Beth intervened. "If he wants to call himself that, he can. I'll order you a fish sandwich, mister, and some fries, too. Want a Coke to go with it?"

"Water'll be fine."

"Jeez." Bobby Earl sniffed. "Probably wants some of that goddamned Perrier or stupid Evian or something."

"Plain water's okay." Michael noted Bobby's pronunciation of Perrier as *Perry-er* and Evian as *E-vee-an.* He was surprised the boy even knew what they were.

"I reckon," Bobby Earl went on, "that Evian spring must be pretty big cause it's in ever stupid store in the whole United States. You yuppie bastards can drink all of it you want."

"Hush up, Bobby Earl."

"It's still stupid."

They ate their food on the way to Lordsburg, Michael doing the best he could with his hands bound. Bobby Earl made Mary Beth take the business exit so he could use a gas station restroom. He was only gone a few minutes, but Michael used the time to try to talk Mary Beth into letting him go.

"I can't do that, mister." She apologized. "Me and Bobby Earl would have to decide that together."

"Did you decide together to kidnap me back in Tucson?"

"No, sir. It was Bobby Earl's idea."

"Then you can let me go."

"No, sir, I better not. 'Sides, we're on our way to get my baby girl in Fort Smith."

"Fort Smith. Is that down in Arkansas somewhere?" Michael didn't really remember the region's geography very well. It had been a long time since he'd been in that part of the country.

"Yes, sir, it's in Arkan… well, you never mind where it is."

"What made you pick me, anyway?"

"Just luck, I reckon."

"Luck?"

"You parked right next to me at that mall there. And we seen you had a lot of money in your billfold."

"Lots of people had money at the mall."

"Yeah, but Bobby Earl seen the way you checked me out, and he wanted me to smile real sweet at you when you came back. I didn't exactly know that we was goin' to take you and your car. Well—maybe your car. And you did have a lot of money."

Over four hundred dollars, Michael reminded himself. He remembered coming out of the mall and walking back to the car. The girl was at the back of their old car. She was smiling and standing with one arm on her hip. Her soft print dress clung to her breasts and hips, and Michael remembered thinking of Faulkner and Dewey Dell from *As I Lay Dying.*

Fecund, that was Faulkner's word for these girls. Child bearers they were. Sexy, women-children whose fecundity could swallow a man right up—and not spit him out. Before Michael had known it, the stupid boy had jumped him and put a pistol in his ribs, and the wild flight from the El Con Mall and Tucson had begun.

"Say," Mary Beth's voice was sweet and friendly, "what kind of professor are you? I mean back at the university. That is where you teach, isn't it?"

"Yes, it is. I teach literature."

"Oh, that must be exciting."

"Yeah, sometimes. It can get boring, though. You'd really have to ask my students."

"You must be awful smart. Me and Bobby Earl, well we never graduated from high school neither one of us."

"Is that when you got married and had the baby?" Michael edged his tied up hands toward the door handle.

"Lord, no." Mary Beth laughed. "Me and Bobby Earl ain't married. I was married to another boy from my hometown. He's my little Marcie Kay's daddy. I met Bobby Earl after I got divorced."

"I'm sorry. That must have been painful. Divorces can really hurt."

"Yes, they can. You have one?"

"No, I haven't." Michael tried to open the back door silently. "But I can imagine."

"It was bad enough."

Mary Beth turned her head to gaze forlornly out the front side window. Michael made his move. He shoved the back door open and pushed himself out, right into Bobby Earl's chest.

"Goin' somewhere, piss face?" The boy dug the .38 into Michaels's ribs where no one else could see it.

"Shit." Michael exhaled deeply.

"Shit is right. You screwed up, teacher boy."

Dragging Michael back into the car behind him, Bobby Earl resumed his position behind the panic-stricken Mary Beth.

"I'm sorry, Bobby Earl, we was just talkin.' I didn't think he would try to get away."

"Shut up." Bobby Earl feinted a backhand at Michael who doubled up and cringed. "Just shut up and drive."

6

BY THE TIME Dave Bishop passed Socorro and was nearing Truth or Consequences, the shadows of the short winter day had lengthened almost to the highway. He had not left Albuquerque immediately as Carol and Ralph no doubt thought he had. Instead, he'd dropped by his house to check on some old files he had there and to pick up the clean little Colt .380 he rarely carried, much less shot. In fact, he'd only fired it at a range a couple of times, but it was a beauty. Light recoil, accurate, easy to handle. He didn't know why he felt he should carry it now, but it was part of the hunch, and he was always one to follow hunches. He found it safer that way.

But now it was getting later in the day, and he hadn't heard from Carol or Ralph, so he decided to find a motel and rest for the night. Make some calls, see what was cooking. He found an inexpensive place on the north end of town, and after getting a bit to eat at their greasy spoon café and resting for a while, he made his phone calls.

He called his mother's place first and was surprised to get her answering machine. Carol must've taken off early to go shopping with her, he thought. He left an "I love you" message for his mom telling her not to worry, he'd be back probably tomorrow, and that he was sorry he had to renege on their shopping date.

"Talk to you soon, Mom." He told the recorder and then hung up.

A call to the office also got a machine. He let Ralph know where he was, the phone number of his room, and to call him if he heard anything on either of their cases.

Stretching and yawning, he turned on the television from the bed. He clicked around the dial a few times with the remote until he landed on a local news broadcast from Las Cruces piped through the cable system at the motel. He had it on for background noise and was half asleep again when the station picked up a live feed from a station out of Tucson. As soon as he heard the word Tucson, Dave popped up wide awake. It was a woman reporter, and she was covering the carjacking scene that had occurred earlier in the day.

Dave filtered out the reporter but greedily absorbed the visual images. They showed where the incident occurred while eyewitnesses talked over the footage, and Dave laughed to see the old junker apparently left behind by the kidnappers. An old rattletrap Chevy. *One for one,* Dave congratulated himself. The next image of interest to Dave was the police artist's sketch of the abductor.

"Bobby Earl, Bobby Earl." He spoke out loud to the room. "Why don't you just announce to the world who you are?" He laughed again and addressed the image on the screen. "Maybe get a haircut, different clothes—never occurs to you, huh, boy crook?"

The report then focused on the victim of the carjacking, with his tearful wife pleading for the criminals to release her husband. Dave edged forward on the bed hoping they would show a picture of the guy. This Michael Wright fellow. And then they did. Dave slapped his legs and let out a hoot.

"Son of a gun. It must be the holiday season. It's two for one night. Two for the price of one. C'mon, baby, just come this way." He leaned back and clapped his hands. "Unbelievable, unfrappin' believable."

7

"THAT WAS A lousy little town." Bobby Earl grumbled when they were back on the interstate leading east away from Lordsburg. "Nothin' but Mexicans. The whole country must've moved up here and took it over or something."

After the outburst it was quiet in the car for a good spell. Mary Beth concentrated on driving, Michael on not doing anything to make Bobby Earl mad, and Bobby Earl on twirling his pistol like a movie outlaw. Then, suddenly, he had an idea.

"Nesto." He exclaimed, pointing the .38 at a sign indicating Deming was the next town coming up. "I just remembered Nesto lives in Deming. We'll get us a cheap motel and hole up for the night there. I'll see if I can get ahold of Nesto."

"Who's Nesto?" Mary Beth glanced at Bobby Earl in the rearview mirror. "Ain't that some kind of Mexican name? I thought you didn't like Mexicans."

"Who said that?" Bobby Earl sniffed. "Me and Nesto did time together in that county jail in Oklahoma. 'Member when I was in there?"

"I don't remember nothin' about no Nesto."

"He's okay. You get up there, take the first exit into that Deming. We'll get a place. I'll call Nesto. He always knows what's up."

"How you gonna get his number?"

"Don't you worry it none. If he's around, I'll find him. I'm lucky that way."

I hope the hell you're not, Michael thought, envisioning what kind of friends Bobby Earl might have made in jail. But less than an hour after they had found a fleabag motel in west Deming, where the manager asked no questions and conducted his business from behind a window made of extremely thick glass, Michael's fears and Bobby Earl's luck were both realized. Michael heard the rumbling of a powerful car engine just outside the motel room, the slamming of two car doors, and then a loud banging on the door. Bobby Earl had Mary Beth get up and open it, and in stepped Nesto.

He was stocky, thick bodied—approximately in his mid-twenties. His coal black hair was barely fuzz cut length, maybe growing back from being shaved. He had on a pair of expensive-looking basketball shoes, dirty, pleated pants, and a T-shirt that revealed several tattoos on his arms and chest—one of which was the *La Raza* symbol Michael associated with the United Farm Workers. Caesar Chavez's old union. Michael had a feeling Nesto hadn't been a member of the UFW.

The new arrival wore the ubiquitous Generation X goatee and had a two or three days' growth of stubble on the rest of his face, which, except for a scar above his left eye, a mean looking mouth, and red, crazy eyes, would have almost been handsome. As it was, he was a tough-looking, scary character. Michael tried to avoid looking directly at him.

Behind and to the side of Nesto appeared a jittery white boy about Bobby Earl's age. He was short and scrawny, wearing greasy blue jeans and a frayed flannel shirt. His face was acne scarred and almost hairless with a crooked nose, thin mouth, and wild, darting eyes. He wore his hair in thin braids like some of the rap artists Michael had sometimes seen when he was surfing through the cable channels in the safety of his home. If Nesto was mean and tough, this guy was sneaky and unstable and very dangerous.

"Who the hell is that?" Bobby Earl wanted to know.

"Hey, good to see you again, too, bro'." Nesto's voice was deep, tinged with the classic accent of a person who had first learned Spanish and then English.

"Who is that?" Bobby Earl's hand hovered over the .38.

"Take it easy, Bobby E." Nesto smiled. "He's cool. He's my partner. Name's Carl D. He just spent too much time with the brothers, that's all. Thinks he's Coolio or something."

Nesto reached out his hand, which Bobby Earl finally shook, all the while looking at Carl D.

"Shit." Bobby Earl pronounced it as *"shee*-it."

"Yo, homes." Carl D. offered his hand. "This is a fly run you be clampin'." Bobby Earl declined the offer. Carl D. shrugged his shoulders.

"What the crap did he just say?"

"Chill, B.E." Nesto raised a hand palm outward. "He just digs whatever action you got goin' here."

"Well, tell him to talk English. I ain't into all that 'brother' bull."

"Whatever, dude," Carl D. drawled. "Y'know what I mean?"

Jesus, Michael prayed to the savior he didn't believe in, *if you'll just get me out of this.*

"So,"—Nesto and Carl D. came on into the room and closed the door behind them—"introduce us to your friends."

"Dig." Carl D. added.

"They ain't my friends. The girl's mine. That turd over there belongs to the car we got outside."

"Holy crap." Nesto shook his head. "You got him in Tucson?"

"How the hell you figure that?"

"We listen to the cop radio out here, bro. They was talking about this carjackin' of some guy in Tucson. Is that you, man? Is that him over there?"

"Maybe." Bobby Earl played it coy. Nesto laughed and smiled at Michael. Carl D. busied himself with checking out Mary Beth. "Hey," Bobby Earl yelled at him, "she's mine. Don't be messin' with her." Carl D. raised both hands in surrender and backed over to a chair by the room's ratty little TV and sat down.

"What's your name?" Nesto turned to Mary Beth.

"Mary Beth." She turned away from Nesto. Across the room, Carl D. messed with the TV dials but kept taking sneak peeks at Mary Beth.

"She's mine," Bobby Earl reiterated.

"We got that," Nesto agreed. "What's the weenie's name over there in the corner?"

"I don't know. I call him Professor. He's some kind of teacher or something. Who gives a big one?"

"His name's Michael." Mary Beth drew brief scrutiny from both Nesto and Bobby Earl.

"Well, Professor Michael,"—Nesto laughed—"you got yourself quite a little classroom here, huh?"

Nesto and Bobby Earl walked over to Michael. Carl D. got up and began edging toward Mary Beth, all the while acting like he was checking out the interior design of the room.

"Whad'ya say, white bread?" Nesto addressed Michael. Michael didn't know what to answer, so he kept his mouth shut. "Why don't you give him to us, man?" Nesto suggested. "We'll take care of him for you."

"Looks like real fresh meat, homes." Carl D.'s eyes were glued on Mary Beth as he got closer and closer to her. "Y'know what I'm sayin'?"

He reached inside a pocket of his flannel shirt and extracted a straight piece of blue glass rounded at one end. Then he dug in the other pocket and came out with a small piece of what looked like murky crystal. He showed them to Mary Beth with a leering smile.

"Bobby, my man." Nesto was negotiating. "I got the most righteous .357 mag. S and W Model 66, four inch barrel. Very cherry. I'll swap it to you for white bread here."

Bobby Earl checked the .38 he had tucked down into his pants. A guy could really blow stuff away with a big .357. The little .38 wasn't diddly. But it was all he could manage at the time.

"I don't know, man."

Michael, the object of the bartering, closed his eyes.

"Naw." Bobby Earl finally declined the offer. "I need him for if the shit comes down."

"If the shit comes down, Bobby, man, they'll waste his ugly ass, too. Don't be foolin' yourself."

"Yeah, but...." Bobby Earl glanced over Nesto's shoulder at Carl D. "Hey, asshole, I done warned you to keep away from her."

"Chill, homes." Carl D. stepped back, prepared to fire up his crack pipe. "Just wanted to see if she was wantin' to get high." Bobby Earl moved at Carl D., but Nesto stepped in the way.

"Calma, Bobby." He put his right hand against Bobby Earl's chest who swept it away with his left. "Sit down," Nesto ordered Carl D. without looking around. Carl D. sat back down by the TV, but he still kept an eye on Mary Beth.

"I'm cool, y'know what I'm sayin'."

"You better stay that way, motherfucker," Bobby Earl threatened.

"Listen, Bobby." Nesto tried to calm him down. "Take it easy. You're upset now. I know this thing's been tough on you. Runnin' the road and all. Tell you what, me and Carl D'll bail for a while. We'll get you some food and drink and stuff. Then we'll come back in a little bit. How's that sound?"

"You can come back."

"Dig. You mind if I bring my 'ho back with me?"

"Guess not."

"All right. What you want? You still eat all that sweet crap?"

"Yeah, get me some pecan twirls and some Orange Slice, man. And some beef jerky, Skoal, and Three Musketeers. Some whiskey and beer. Here." He offered Nesto a couple of Michael's twenties.

"On me, brother. You're the guest in my town."

"Su casa es mi casa, know what I'm sayin'." Carl D. added.

"Shut up, C.D."

"Chillin', bro." Carl D. winked at Mary Beth.

"I'll bring that stuff later, Bobby," Nesto grabbed Carl D. and herded him toward the door. "Just relax, order a pizza or something to hold you over. I'll be back later."

"All right. Thanks, Nesto."

"Mas tarde."

Nesto headed out, pushing jabbering Carl D. out the door.

"Yo, homes. It was a fly groove jawin' at you, know what I'm sayin'."

"See ya, Bobby Earl." Nesto closed the door.

Michael let his breath out when the two men were gone.

"Crazy, rap-talkin' piece of shit." Bobby Earl kept looking at the closed door. "Stupid bastard."

WHEN NESTO RETURNED later in the evening, he came with a trashy-looking girl he introduced as Mona, carrying a big bag of junk food groceries, and wearing the .357 he had talked about earlier in a shoulder holster under a light jacket. During his absence, Mary Beth had ordered pizza for all of them, one-half veggie for Michael over Bobby Earl's vehement objections.

After they had eaten, Bobby Earl made sure Michael's hands and feet were bound securely, and then he sat the teacher against a back wall in the hotel room. For Michael this was a distinct improvement over being face to face with the boy and his .38 in the bathroom, which was where they'd hustled him when the pizza kid had arrived.

Now, late in the evening, with Bobby Earl, Nesto, and the girl Mona sitting at the room's small table drinking whisky and tequila, smoking cigarettes, and playing cards, Michael—despite the constant jangling of his fear-stimulated nerves or perhaps because of them—began to drift off.

He slipped into an odd state between sleeping and waking, and his mind pummeled him with unbidden and unwanted thoughts. He went through a hierarchy of blame, from Barbara to the University of Arizona to God. But the hierarchy always ended at the same place—with him, Michael Wright.

In the last few years, he'd made an effort to work on his piece of this picture—tried to accept some responsibility for his own life. Despite the things he'd done in the past. Despite—and the image of an explosion forced its way into his consciousness, with the flames, the broken glass, the splintered wood all too clear—despite that one thing, the one thing so long ago.

He had to take personal responsibility for it, for himself. But consider the situation he was in now. Did he want to be in it? Did he choose this? Of course not, he had simply been stupid and unobservant.

Now he was paying for it. And then, in a flash of crisp lucidity, it occurred to him that he was more than a little bit crazy. Not Looney Tunes nuts or psychotic but slightly off, a shade out there, not fully with it. And why? Because almost every major drive in his life had been thwarted. He had become—and maybe had always been—out of synch with the world. If he was edging up on wacko, well it was....

"Michael, Michael." A voice broke into his near dream-state thoughts. He imagined briefly that it was Barbara waking him because he'd overslept. He smiled, thinking he was in his comfortable bed back in Tucson. But the voice was more insistent than Barbara's, different. "Professor, wake up. Michael." He opened his eyes to see Mary Beth bent over him, her face directly in front of his.

"What, what?" He whipped his head around to locate Bobby Earl, but the boy and the others weren't there. He and the girl were the only ones in the room. The fear abated, but his heart still pounded.

"Take it easy. They're gone. That Nesto and his girlfriend left. Bobby went out with them for a minute. I was just seein' how you was feelin'."

"Oh."

"Are you all right?" Mary Beth's face was still close to his.

"Yes, thank you."

"I'm awful sorry about everything."

"He's going to have to kill me, isn't he?" Michael focused on the girl's cool, light green eyes.

"Now hush that talk up," she scolded, putting her hand gently on his arm. "No such thing's goin' to happen."

"You wouldn't hurt me, would you?"

"Of course not." Her tone reminded Michael of how his grade school teachers used to talk to the little kids. Benevolent but sometimes amused by the child's naiveté and lack of understanding. He felt a testosterone driven twitch in his crotch. "But please don't try to run away anymore until Bobby Earl decides it's okay to let you go, all right?"

"Why don't you let me go?"

"I can't."

"Why not?" Michael gazed intently into the girl's appealing face.

They were close together now, mouths only inches apart. Michael fought a powerful urge to lean forward and kiss the girl's soft lips. Mary Beth leaned slightly toward him as well. Her breathing was shallow, and her words came out slowly.

"I can't… I…."

Suddenly the door banged open, and Bobby Earl was standing there. Mary Beth quickly drew back and stood up. Michael stared down at the floor as if looking for something he'd lost.

"What the hell's goin' on here?" Bobby Earl boomed. "What are you two doin'?"

"N—nothing." Michael glanced up sideways at the boy.

"I was just seein' how he was." Mary Beth explained.

"Oh, is that all?" Bobby Earl stepped fully into the room and slammed the door shut behind him.

"That's all, sweetheart." Mary Beth went over to him. He pushed her away.

"Bull, you was gettin' ready to hump him."

"No, I wasn't."

"No, really." Michael interjected. "She wasn't. I swear. We weren't doing anything."

"Shut up." Mary Beth tried to put her arms around the boy to comfort him. "Get off me." He grabbed her arm and threw her toward the bed. Then he went for Michael. "You stupid butthole." He gave Michael a sharp kick to the ribs.

Michael cried out and fell over, raising his bound hands to protect himself. Bobby Earl reached down and slapped him hard across the face. Michael curled up in a ball, groaning, eyes tearing from the slap.

"Stop it, Bobby Earl," Mary Beth yelled from the bed. Bobby Earl turned toward her.

"You want some of it, do ya?"

"Bobby." Mary Beth backed away on her knees toward the headboard. "Bobby Earl."

"Lay down."

"Bobby, I don't wanna."

"Down!" Mary Beth lay down. "Roll over."

"I don't want to do it that way, honey."

"Roll over."

"Not in front of him."

"Screw him." Bobby Earl was already taking down his pants. Michael had gotten himself back to a sitting position but wouldn't look over at the couple.

"Please, baby. Please."

"Turn over."

"You know I don't like it back there, Bobby Earl. Easy, baby."

"I'll easy it all right." He almost tore off the girl's underpants.

"Please, baby, not in front of Michael. Oh. Ow."

"Michael? Michael can go to hell. He's lucky I don't do this to him."

"Don't say that." Mary Beth panted between Bobby Earl's hard, frenzied thrusts.

"Maybe I'll let Nesto and that crazy, white rap ass have some of him tomorrow, the yuppie bastard."

"Oh, Bobby." Mary Beth sobbed. "That hurts me." Bobby Earl grunted louder, above Mary Beth's whimpering.

His own body compacted into a virtual, sitting fetal position, Michael fought to block out the sounds in the room. His body shook against his will, and he wished that anything else in the world than this could be happening to him. He wished it would all go away. He wished he were dead.

8

DAVE BISHOP WOKE up late. The sun was already well above the eastern horizon, and its rays beamed through a crack in the heavy motel room curtains, hitting him right in the eyes.

"Son of a gun." He flung back the bedsheets and sat bolt upright. "I overslept."

He checked his watch where he'd laid it on the nightstand. Nine thirty. He checked it again. Same time. He had slept later than he had in years. Why? Then he remembered that he had been unable to sleep the night before. After the newscast with the picture of the kidnapped man, Dave's mind had begun to race—race with old memories that came back to him at an overwhelming speed.

Columbia, Missouri, 1969. He had been a neophyte student cop, talked into working undercover inside the local student political organizations by an FBI agent who had mentored the impressionable young man. Dave had become a political narc, posing as a radical member of the SDS Weathermen.

The FBI had given him a very thorough fake background—demonstrations, grass roots organizing credentials, even a bogus trip to Cuba with the Venceremos Brigades. Chopping cane in Cuba—that was a good one. But Dave had been dedicated, a true believer, and he made the assignment succeed, working his way further and further into the local, vociferous student political groups. That's when he had met Michael Wyche. Michael Wright now, that is.

Dave had worked hard to gain Michael's trust and that of his political friends. He partied with them, smoked dope with them, dropped acid. He was quick to espouse half-baked leftist ideas, passed himself off as some sort of neo-Marxist Trotskyite—whatever the hell that was. But all the time he was intelligence-gathering for school and local authorities, for his buddy at the FBI.

Finally, in the spring of 1970, when campuses around the country went completely mad over the Kent State killings, Michael's group got so radical—they hatched a plan to attack the local draft board and disrupt on-campus ROTC activities, with whatever means necessary—that Dave called the people he worked for. But somebody in the movement was ahead of him and the game, and the main leaders of the planned action went—as the old saying goes—on the lam. Police rounded up all the pawns, but the big players vanished, left campus, disappeared, went truly underground.

Dave's cover was blown, then, but he had been such a good soldier and done such a good job that he made it into the real FBI. For the next couple of years he was based out of the St. Louis office, tracking down the Missouri radicals who had slipped from his grasp. He found two of them—one in Mississippi, one in Michigan—and one turned herself in. The other one he had been hot after, Michael Wyche, was harder to catch. But Dave traced him to Boulder, Colorado, then to Memphis, and finally, in a near miss, lost him in a nighttime border crossing in Laredo, Texas. Michael Wyche crossed the bridge into Nuevo Laredo and vanished into old Mexico.

Dave kept Wyche's file open—mostly as a reminder to himself of his arm's length failure in apprehending the fugitive. When he quit the FBI to take a detective job with the Albuquerque PD, Dave had surreptitiously copied the Wyche file, though he never thought anything would come of it, and he had not thought about the case for some time. Until last night. Now he had found Michael Wyche again. After all these years. And the poor bastard had had the tables turned on him. Now he'd been kidnapped by this lowlife Bunton character, a real piece of work.

Oh, well, Dave thought, calling Ralph's phone, *that's the way things go.* Real life was always wilder, more coincidental, more amazing than fiction could ever be. The chickens had come home to roost for Michael Wright, *nee* Wyche. After all this time. Karma, these Wyche/Wright types would say. Not instant Karma, certainly, but Karma, nonetheless.

"Any word overnight, Ralphie Boy?" Dave bypassed the front office phone. He didn't want to talk to Carol just yet and hear how his mother was probably annoyed with him for breaking another shopping date with her.

"Zero. They must have holed up somewhere."

"Uh-huh." Dave grunted.

"The last sighting was still on I-10. Maybe they made it to Las Cruces or even El Paso."

"Or maybe only to Deming or Lordsburg. What about the road between Deming and Hatch?"

"26, you mean?"

"Yeah."

"Nothing that's come in. The immigration boys are on that road pretty often. They would probably have seen our perps."

"If they're still together and if they're still in the same vehicle."

"You got something?"

"No."

"Dave?" Ralph's tone was slightly doubtful. *"You holding out something on me?"*

"No. No way."

Dave didn't like leaving Ralph in the dark like this, but this Wyche, er, Wright guy was his own little secret for now. Hell, maybe the guy wasn't the same person after all. It had been a long time.

"Dave?" Ralph's voice insisted on the other end of the line.

"Sorry, buddy. Nothin' but a hunch. I just have a feeling about this Bunton kid. I don't think they're that far way."

"Well, if you do find him, call for backup. Don't be a hero."

"Not me." Dave laughed.

"Okay."

"You keep me posted during the day?"

"You have the car phone, right?"

"Got it," Dave confirmed. "Call me if anything breaks."

"All right."

"Anything. I'll be heading south."

"Got you, bud."

9

MICHAEL WRIGHT WOKE hurting, his wrists chafed from where Bobby Earl had roughly tightened the cord around them the night before. His usual headache was back, and back with a vengeance. Sunlight filtered through a crack in the window drapes, a narrow beam crossing the bed where the boy and girl lay sleeping. Michael wanted to get up, bound as he was, and make a break for it, but he couldn't. He was too tired, his head throbbed too much, and actually—strangely—he didn't care.

What would it matter if these two killed him? You had to die some time, some way. What was the difference if it was this way? It wasn't like he was an innocent lamb being led to the slaughter. It wasn't like his life was going to make a difference to anybody. It wasn't like he would be missed. For some reason Dostoevski's *Raskolnikov* popped into his head.

Guilt, that was it. We were all guilty, whether of a specific crime or not, and we were going to pay for it. One way or another, somehow, we would pay for all the bad things we'd done in our lives, if only with our deaths. God, or fate or destiny, or karma, or whatever it was, would see to that. There could be no other resolution, no compromise, no accommodation. There were, after all, no happy endings.

Then, in a flash of clarity that penetrated his foggy, aching brain,

Michael realized the full extent of the failure that was his life. Always out of step. Never in proper sync. Apostate, dissident. Odd terms for describing people who couldn't quite fit into a given society. People who wouldn't accept things as they were. People who were confused, afraid. Living lives of agonizingly quiet desperation, except for an occasional outburst of temper, a vocal objection, an act of disobedience.

That's maybe what he, Michael Wright, was—or had been—but what were people like Bobby Earl, Nesto, and Carl D.? And Mary Beth? The boys were rebels, outlaws, bandits—with or without a cause. But Mary Beth—she didn't fit in to any of this. She just wanted to be home, with her family, with her baby.

Holy hell, he inwardly chastised himself, *what am I doing? I'm slipping into that Stockholm Syndrome, or whatever it was called. I'm starting to become a hostage. Seeing the kidnappers' point of view. What a load of crap. I have to get out of here.*

Drawing himself up to his knees, he tried loosening the cord that bound his hands behind his back. He could almost reach the knot but not quite. His fingers were just not long enough or strong enough to manipulate it. Careful not to make any noise, he leaned against the back wall and managed to stand. He shuffled over to the bathroom and turned his body so that he could reach his hands out as far as possible. He was able to turn the doorknob.

Quietly then, moving as softly as he possibly could, he slowly approached the front door. Turning to his right, he maneuvered his hands onto the doorknob. On the first try, they slipped, and the knob spun back with a click. He tried a second time, then a third. On the fourth try, he got his hands on the knob firmly. He began to turn the knob. Suddenly, there was a loud banging on the door. He almost fell back onto the bed where the boy and girl lay.

"Jesus." He cried out. The banging on the door continued.

"Wha...?" Bobby Earl mumbled, coming awake, sleepy-eyed. "What the hell?" The banging persisted. Michael tried to hurry back across the room. "Where you goin'?" He heard the boy cry out behind him.

"What's going on?" Mary Beth sat up in bed yawning.

"See who's at the door. I gotta take care of weenie boy over there. He was doin' somethin' weird."

"No." Michael looked toward the bed. Bobby Earl bounded out, naked, and was on him immediately.

"Answer the door," the boy ordered Mary Beth again. He stuck the .38 right against Michael's jaw. "If it's the cops, the prof is roadkill."

"W—who's there?" Mary Beth called out, hands against the door.

"Look out and see," Bobby Earl yelled.

"Hey, open up," a man's voice from outside.

"It's that Nesto. With his girlfriend."

"Okay. Give me a minute, and let 'em in. You get over against the wall, piss ant." Michael slid down against the baseboard.

"Just a second," Mary Beth hollered to the people outside the room. "We ain't decent yet." Michael could hear muffled laughter from outside.

"Hey, dude." Nesto had a big grin when he and his girlfriend were let in a couple of minutes later. "What is this, you so rich now you sleep all day, homes?"

"What time is it?" Bobby Earl had put on blue jeans and another black T-shirt. This one had White Zombie on it. Michael wondered, is there no end to these damned bands?

"Man, it must be after ten, dude, you know. Ain't that right, Mona?" Nesto laughed.

Mona snarled something in Spanish.

"Puta."

"Cabrón." She spat back.

Nesto laughed again.

"What's the deal? I didn't expect to see you no more."

"Dig, B. E. We brought you another bunch of your sweet goodies and stuff out in the car, and I got a plan for you, too."

"A plan?" Bobby Earl tucked in his T-shirt. "Mary Beth, you wanna get us somethin' to eat and drink?"

"Sure."

"I'll help you," Mona offered.

"Thanks."

The two girls busied themselves making instant coffee and putting together a breakfast out of the junk food left from the night before.

"What's this plan, Nesto? Not another trade for the prof there?" He pointed the .38 at Michael, who lowered his head to his knees and tried to act as calm as he could under the circumstances.

"Naw, you can keep his punk ass. I got a different trade for you."

"Yeah?"

"Check this. White bread's car there is hot, no? The cops'll be lookin' all over for it."

"So?"

"So, I got me a bitchin' Buick outside. New primer coat, new engine. A cherry machine."

"Uh-huh."

"Well, hell, man, we trade. I'll swap the hot car over in Mexico and make some dough. You got a fast getaway car nobody knows about."

"Here, y'all." Mary Beth and Mona handed cups of hot coffee to the men.

"I don't want that." Bobby Earl pushed his away. "Ain't there some more Orange Slice?"

"Yeah, but it ain't cold."

"Go get some ice," Bobby Earl ordered. "Both of you."

"Go ahead," Nesto told Mona.

"That ain't enough." Bobby Earl waited until the girls had gone out.

"Don't be greedy, brother. There's another bag of goodies out there, man. I got some good stuff, too, if you want it. Weed, crack, crank, crystal meth—whatever, you name it."

"That ain't what I want."

"What else I got… oh, I see."

"That, too."

"You want the piece."

"I want the piece."

Nesto unzipped the light Oakland Raiders jacket he was wearing. Reaching in slowly, he unsnapped a couple of buttons and pulled out the shoulder holster containing the shiny, stainless steel .357 revolver. He reached it across to Bobby Earl.

"Deal?" Bobby Earl fingered the weapon greedily.

"Deal." The boy laughed with nearly childish joy. "Hot damn deal."

Nesto laughed, too, and slapped hands with Bobby Earl.

Across the room, Michael closed his eyes and tried to imagine himself somewhere else, anywhere else. He tried but couldn't. He was caught in a surreal web of time, space, and circumstance. And there was nothing for it, nothing to do. Except wait. Wait for fate or chance to take a hand. Stay cool and don't do anything stupid. Wait for whatever opportunity might present itself. *Empty yourself of all hope, need, desire. Just wait.*

10

DAVE BISHOP TOOK the Highway 26 cutoff at Hatch and headed cross desert for Deming on another of his hunches. He knew both Bobby Earl Bunton and the fugitive ex-radical that the punk hoodlum had carjacked out of Tucson. It was definitely a police, even FBI, case now, but Dave felt he had the inside track on all of them. He felt he could find this little traveling side show all on his own.

He had trailed Bobby Earl before, as well as the man now known as Michael Wright, and if he kept his ear to the metaphorical road, there was a good chance he might come up on them first. Dangerous as that might be, both personally and professionally, Dave liked the idea. Two birds with one stone.

It would give him a real sense of accomplishment, of closure as they said nowadays. Months of chasing the one guy, decades on the other. Hell, it sounded like a retirement run to Dave, even if he wasn't quite old enough for that yet. With a chuckle, he called up Ralph on to see if there was anything new on the wires or from police sources.

"Still nothing new."

"Well, keep at it and keep me posted."

"Will do."

Dave drove on toward Deming, memories of Michael Wyche and old University of Missouri days flitting through his mind. He had actually grown to like most of the students he was narcing on back then. Generally, they were intelligent, idealistic, energetic. But they finally went too far. At least as far as the FBI and the U.S. government were concerned. An inner group of the radicals, including Michael Wyche, now Wright, had hatched a plan to blow up or burn down the local draft board as well as anything related to the ROTC program on campus.

He would never forget the confused, betrayed looks on the faces of the kids who they'd busted when he led the FBI to their clandestine, pre-attack meeting. Perhaps they saw the same look in Dave's eyes when none of the four leaders—Michael among them—had been at this most critical gathering. Someone had burned Dave, too, and this group of revolutionary pawns, if you will, took the fall for their leaders.

The whole incident stuck in Dave's craw. Not so much because the leaders had slipped through his fingers, although that was very annoying in itself, but because he didn't know who had turned him in the deal, warning the students ahead of time. So when he was offered a job by the Feds, he jumped at it and for a few years was able to channel his energies in tracking down the elusive radical foursome. And they all fell, one by one—except for Wyche.

He remembered getting the phone tip that Michael was making a run for Mexico, even down to the port of exit—Laredo. He recalled waiting at that long bridge all one day and into the evening. The next morning in the hubbub of people crossing in both directions—tourists to waste their money on Mexican trinkets, Mexicans coming over to work in the higher paying menial jobs no sensible Texan would take—in all that movement of humanity, Dave checked every single hippie-ish looking man, woman, or child who crossed the border.

Then around ten a.m. a taxi drove across, stopping at the Mexican side for the authorities to check it out. Dave sidled over by the vehicle, saw three men in the car besides the driver. There was a middle-aged Mexican man up front and two men in suits in the back. The one nearest him in back of the car was Mexican, the other a *gringo*. They were clean shaven, smelling of cheap cologne. The *gringo* had blonde hair and wore a dark business hat pulled down low on his head. He looked straight ahead the whole time.

The Mexican guards let the vehicle pass, and though something was gnawing at him, Dave made no effort to stop the vehicle. He watched it go into Mexico, following it with his eyes as it went west, then turned south to head into the heart of Nuevo Laredo. Just before the taxi disappeared, an arm came out of the back right rider's window. The hand was extended with the middle finger stuck up into the air.

"Son of a bitch." Dave knew he'd been had. "Damn it."

And so the student radical, Michael Wyche, had faded into the Mexican countryside. He must've stayed in Nuevo Laredo for some time because he never appeared at the watched airport, nor the bus or train stations. In a few weeks, the search was dropped, and Wyche slipped into that big bucket of 60s radicals and activists who were swallowed up by the forgetful 70s and the self-absorbed 80s and 90s.

Out of view until now, in a new millennium when a crazed loser boy had pulled the poor bugger kicking and screaming, as it were, back into the spotlight. Still, Dave figured he was probably the only guy in the region, if not the entire country, who knew who Michael Wright, nee Wyche, really was and for sure the only one who cared—if he actually even still did so himself.

"We'll see." He spoke out loud and then checked the rearview mirror. He took a deep breath. "Holy crap."

Coming up fast from behind was a police car, probably the highway patrol, its lights flashing. He searched for the nearest safe place to pull over and had barely gotten off the road when the vehicle roared by, siren blaring. It was a New Mexico Highway Patrolman.

"Probably after our very boys." Dave pulled back onto the highway. "I don't wish you too good luck." The patrol car was nearly out of sight already. "Prefer to end this hunt myself."

A few miles down the road, he approached a short series of turns and dips in the mostly straight highway. As he was coming out of the last curve where the road angled off in a more direct, southerly direction for a good long stretch, a large gray car, mid-70s Pontiac or Olds,

Dave guessed—some bomb of a gas hog at any rate—suddenly pulled out of a gravel parking lot on the right hand side of the road and recklessly crossed over the highway toward him.

He slowed to make sure the other vehicle had settled onto its side of the road, and the two cars passed each other, the big car rumbling by with a girl at the wheel. Dave watched the vehicle in his rearview mirror as it sped away, shortly rounding the curve behind him and disappearing quickly from sight.

"Boy, they were haulin' A."

In seconds, he reached the parking lot from where the gray car had emerged. The back windows had been darkly tinted, and he had not been able to see who, if anyone, had been in the back seat. Yet he had the impression, or feeling, that there were other people in the car besides the girl.

Slowing up, he glanced over from where the car had shot out. It was a parking lot for an isolated bar and grill out in the middle of—well, that was exactly what it was called—the Middle of Nowhere Bar. Laughing, Dave hit the gas and sped on toward Deming. He checked his rearview mirror again, then back to the front. There wasn't another car on the entire part of the highway he could see in either direction.

11

NESTO, MONA, AND CARL D. were doing tequila shooters in the Black Cat bar on a dusty side street in Deming. They had parked Michael's Honda in front of the bar—nobody came to the Black Cat except heavy drinkers and the few dopers in town—and they now sat in a rundown booth in a dark corner of the place deciding what to do.

"Check it out, bro." Carl D.'s hands moved in all directions as he spoke. "We gotta ditch that white bread ride quick, dig me, dude? You know what I'm sayin'? Let's split for the border."

Nesto laughed at Carl D.'s discomfort. For a boy who'd done as much time as he had, he was remarkably nervous out here in the real world. "Take it easy, C.D. We have a nice lunch here, drink us some more tequila, and then we'll run that baby through Naco later. With me, dude?"

"Mejór que vamos ahora." Mona didn't like any of this swapping cars with that crazy white boy at the motel. And she let Nesto know as much. Very plainly.

"Calma, baby. Tranquilate. Everything's cool." Nesto reached his arm for Mona, but she pushed it away. "Women."

"I'm with her." Carl D. nodded his head up and down.

"You'd like to be." Nesto snorted, then called to the bartender. "Hey, Rudy, we get some burritos over here?"

"We only got hamburger and egg ones," Rudy called back.

"Give us four, no, five. Lots of red sauce."

"Oralé." Rudy went about the business of heating the frozen burritos in a food-stained microwave at the far end of the bar.

Nesto poured more tequila a few minutes later. "Hey, Rudy, what's up? What are you doing over there? I'm starvin'."

Rudy came out from behind the bar and peered out the one greasy window in the front of the Black Cat.

"Nesto. What kind of car you drivin' today?"

"What you talkin' about?" Nesto sensed trouble and began to rise. The girl, Mona, blissfully downed another shooter.

"There's cops out here looking at a gray Honda in front." Rudy checked out the window. "I thought you had a big old Pontiac or Buick or something."

"It ain't mine if the cops are lookin' at it."

"That mother burnt us." Carl D. jumped up. "Bobby Earl. Bastard."

"We don't know that, dude."

"They're opening the doors on it." Rudy peered through the glass at the police. "Is this the one you were driving?"

"Not mine," Nesto repeated, pointing to the back door of the bar and holding up an index finger to his mouth to silence Carl D. and Mona. "You know I got that old Buick."

"Oh, yeah." Rudy kept looking out. "Gray primer one. I remember."

The microwave dinged, and Rudy tore himself away from watching the cops. He took out the burritos, put them on a big plate, then grabbed a bowl of not very sanitary looking red sauce.

"Here you go." He turned toward the other end of the bar. "Hey, what the…?"

The place was empty. The customers had all sneaked out, apparently through the back door.

"Well, I'll be"—Rudy shook his head—"if that don't beat all."

12

BOBBY EARL FELL asleep just a few miles outside Deming on the way to Hatch. He had chosen Highway 26 because he figured it was a road nobody would take much, and they had hardly gotten on the road before the boy started to doze. He fought it at first, worried that the stupid college boy would try something, but after a few minutes he slid into that middle ground between sleeping and waking. The last things he remembered seeing were a crappy looking apartment building on the right side of the road just outside Deming and then a little farther up on the left a rock hound place that was closed down. Eyes closing heavily against his will, Bobby Earl went out.

And he dreamed. Fitfully. Dreamed of being a kid again. Of working on the farm with the old man. He was tagging along, following close behind his dad, skipping along. The old man was cussing as usual, but he would stop every little bit to fix some loose barbed wire on the fence or prop up a scrawny, rotting fence post. Bobby Earl laughed when the old man swore and then got so close that he accidentally bumped into him. The old man spun around, eyes and face red, mouth twisted in anger, and pushed him down.

But the boy got up and followed on. Still close. Every few steps, the old man would push him back, but the boy would jump up each time, dust himself off, and run up to his father again. Then the boy saw it sticking out of a back pocket in the old man's overalls. It had a shiny copper colored cap and was dark brown, just the cap and the top edge showed.

"What's this, Daddy? What's this, Daddy?"

"Never you mind what it is, dumbhead." The old man growled and grabbed the bottle. He pulled it out and took a big drink.

"Dumbhead, dumbhead, dumbhead." The boy sang, and the old man shoved him down again.

The boy got up. The old man shoved him down again. Up once more. And then the old man slapped him. Stinging sharp at first, then harder. The boy tried to cover up. Made a feeble attempt to hit back. That made the old man hit harder. With his fists then. Once, twice. The boy was on the ground screaming, crying. Blood ran out of his nose and mouth, and the old man kept hitting him. Hitting him.

"Stop it, you old bastard." Bobby Earl cried out from his dream, waking himself. "Where are we?"

Mary Beth checked him out in the rearview mirror. The stupid professor scrunched back as far as he could get from him in the back seat. If Bobby Earl hadn't been feeling so confused, sleepy, and mad from the dream, he would have laughed at the wimpy college man.

"Are you all right, baby?" Mary Beth asked in that goody-goody voice of hers that Bobby Earl hated. "You was sleepin'. Must've had a bad dream. A nightmare or somethin'."

"Where the hell are we, I ast ya." Bobby Earl slurred, fighting a yawn.

"We must be about halfway or so to that next town up ahead. You was only asleep for a little while really."

"Really." Bobby Earl imitated Mary Beth's mealy mouthed woman's way of talking.

"There's no need to snap at me."

"Just shut up and drive. I gotta get my head straight. Let me think a minute."

"What about?"

"I said drive."

"Okay, okay."

Bobby Earl rubbed his scraggly, stubby chin and studied the passing countryside. Dark hills off to the right, rolling scrub land on the left. Ahead, the road stretched straight out to a curve at the horizon. The closer they got to that curve, the more a funny feeling grew inside him. This road was too empty.

"What are them buildings up there?" He leaned across the back seat next to Mary Beth.

"Where, Bobby?"

"There on the left, by the curve."

"I can't make it out just yet."

"Slow up."

Mary Beth eased off the gas as they neared the buildings. To the left was a trailer with a couple of dogs in the yard and some old cars and trucks by the fence surrounding it. Straight off the road, if you didn't take the curve, was a flat one-floor building butted up against the rocky, sandy wall of the desert.

"I'll be." Bobby Earl laughed. "Pull over in there. Put the car as far back from the road as you can."

Mary Beth did as she was told. The tires made a snapping, cracking sound as they crossed slowly over the rocky gravel parking lot leading up to the low flat building.

"Don't that beat the hell out of all. The Middle of Nowhere Bar. At least they got that right, by God. We're sure as hell in the middle of nowhere right enough."

"We gonna get somethin' to eat, Bobby?"

"Not just yet, baby...." Bobby Earl began, then held up his hand. "Shh, listen."

"What?"

"Just shut up." Bobby Earl snarled. "Leave the engine on. Let it idle. And listen."

Mary Beth and Michael both listened intently, but they heard nothing. At first. But then came the familiar sound. Low at first, then louder, louder.

"Police!" Michael exclaimed.

"Shut up, butthead." Bobby Earl feinted an elbow at Michael. Michael shut up.

The siren grew louder, louder, then whined by as the Highway Patrol car zoomed by on the way to Deming. Mary Beth and Michael sat in tension-locked silence. Bobby Earl reached forward and turned the rearview mirror where he could watch the cop car. It grew smaller and smaller, siren no longer audible, flashing lights now distant, strobing pinholes of color. He flopped back into the rear seat. Michael released a pent-up sigh. Mary Beth readjusted the rearview mirror.

"Get us the hell out of here," Bobby Earl commanded. "And hammer it."

13

DAVE BISHOP WAS almost to Deming when he got a call from Ralph Ortega back in Albuquerque.

"What's up, Ralphie." He pressed the speakerphone button.

Dave hated all the idiots driving around the country nowadays with one hand on the steering wheel and the other holding a phone. He figured about one out of every fifty of them had any kind of reason at all to be talking on the phone and driving at the same time. Safety hazards were all they were. Maybe the cops ought to stop having DWI roadblocks and make them phone-in-the-car stops instead. Phone talking drivers had to be as dangerous as a guy with a couple of beers in his belly—at least.

"Got some new hot poop for you, old buddy." Dave could tell his partner had something good, the upbeat tone in his normally taciturn voice gave him away.

"Shoot."

"Okay. Deming police report they found the victim's car, the gray Honda."

"No kidding?"

"No kidding. They got an anonymous call that the victim's car was abandoned in front of some lowlife bar there in Deming."

"Sounds like Bobby Earl's kind of place all right. What about our boy and his 'guest?'"

"That's the good part. Nobody seen 'em, but the anonymous source believes there was a trade of some kind. He didn't say how he knew that, but he had a description of the possible trade-off car."

"And?" Dave waited for Ralph's big finish.

"A classic vato *car, man. Early seventies Buick. Big, old, rebuilt. And painted primer gray."*

"What?" Dave nearly yelled, hitting the brakes.

"Seventy-something Buick, restored, with gray primer color."

"Stupid." Dave scolded himself for not paying enough attention to things.

"What's up, partner?"

"I passed a car like that probably not a half hour ago or less."

"Think it could be them?"

"Most likely. Oh, crap!"

"What now?"

"I've got to get gas. I'm almost to Deming. I'll fill up there and then head back to Hatch. Keep me up on any more info as it comes in."

"Want me to meet you in Socorro?"

"No. Just stand by. This thing may be coming to a head."

"You call me, I'll be there."

"Gotcha, buddy. Talk to you later. And thanks."

"You're welcome. And play it safe down there, Dave."

"Later, partner."

"Later."

14

MICHAEL COWERED IN his corner of the back seat while Mary Beth tore out of the Middle of Nowhere's parking lot back onto Highway 26.

"Jesus Christ, Mary Beth," Bobby Earl yelled as the girl brought the weaving Buick under control in time to avoid a near miss with an oncoming light blue, late model Ford Taurus. The Ford had braked to ensure that there was room enough for the two cars to pass one another on the otherwise now empty highway. "You nearly hit that stupid car."

"Be quiet, Bobby Earl," Mary Beth yelled back, voice quavering.

Michael thought the girl was about to start crying. And no wonder. The boy treated her scarcely better, if at all, than he did Michael, whom he had kidnapped. But vicious as the boy was, Michael had to admit that Bobby Earl had a remarkable sense of impending danger. A sixth sense that amazed Michael and truly did remind him of the outlaws the boy had mentioned earlier, depression-era thieves and killers like Pretty Boy Floyd, John Dillinger, and Clyde Barrow.

Earlier, Michael had banked on the boy's heightened senses not working, at least while he slept, because he had again tried to find a way to reach the girl while Bobby Earl dozed. He hoped the young tough hadn't somehow managed to absorb what he and the girl had talked about, even while apparently sleeping.

"How long have you two been a couple?" Michael asked Mary Beth softly when Bobby Earl dropped off just outside Deming.

Mary Beth checked in the rearview mirror, saw the boy's head angled against the back seat, his breath coming in a long, regular pattern. She answered in a near whisper.

"A good spell now, maybe a year or so."

"Does he treat you good?"

"Sometimes."

"I think he treats you terribly."

"He don't always. You just seen him at his worst."

"I suppose."

"Well, it's not like how that poor woman got treated in that book Color something."

"You mean *The Color Purple?"* Michael was surprised the girl had read anything at all. "You read that book?"

"Yes."

"And you liked it?"

"It was awful real to me. Do you know it?"

"Yes."

"Wadn't it good?"

"In a politically correct sense, I suppose." Michael was never able to control his teacher side. He was thinking how far this current glut of literary treatments of domestic violence were from the thematic depth of people like Dostoevski, Tolstoi, Garcia-Marquez, Hemingway, Flannery O'Connor.

"What does that mean, politically correct?"

"To me it means we all have to share the same attitudes about social issues, political goals, and ideals."

"Like what, for instance?" Michael watched Bobby Earl to make sure he was still asleep.

"Like peace and drugs and abortion, stuff like that."

"I wouldn't want to have an abortion. Would you?"

"I won't ever have to."

"You know what I mean. You wouldn't want your wife to have one, would you?"

"I might. It would depend."

"You don't have children, do you?" It was like a light had gone on for Mary Beth.

"No."

"Then you don't believe in miracles."

"What?"

"Birth. Havin' a baby. That's a miracle, mister."

"There are about five or six billion miracles walking around the earth right now, you know."

"Oh, my. You college folk. Did your wife have one of them without telling you?" Michael was silent as a flood of old memories poured into his consciousness. "That's awful."

Michael wanted to tell her it wasn't awful, that he had wanted the abortion more than his wife even, but the girl spoke again.

"I tell you what, Michael." The girl spoke so sincerely and so sweetly Michael felt a part of himself go over to her unconditionally. "If you was my man, I'd a asked you first. And you'd be a daddy right now."

Michael slumped back in the seat. All his existential walls amounted to nothing here. This girl, for all her ignorance and her bad judgment, was remarkable. She had that something Michael, and perhaps most people, had lost somewhere along the way. Hope. And perhaps even more significantly, potential.

Mary Beth could improve. She had the heart for it. Down deep she was what he used to call a really good person. She deserved better than what she had. She deserved a break, a chance in life. He leaned forward to tell her so, and then the boy woke up. Mumbling from some dream he must have been having, then, as usual, screaming at the girl.

"Where are we?"

Michael closed his eyes and leaned against the door as far from Bobby Earl as he could get. He let Mary Beth deal with this crazed boy. She was probably the only one in the world who could.

15

DAVE BISHOP RETRACED his route from Deming to Hatch, inwardly chastising himself all the way for not realizing he had driven right by the fugitive kidnappers in their newly obtained—God only knew how—big old primer gray Buick. And now he remembered that Ralph had mentioned there might be a woman involved. A woman. How stupid of him not to put two and two together. She was no doubt the one he'd seen driving the car he nearly crashed into on the highway before.

When he reached Hatch, making the left off the main strip of the tiny town to head over to I-25, Dave decided to stop at a convenience store just up from the corner on the west side of the road. Shutting off the Taurus, he went inside to get something to drink and to check with the clerk, just in case.

"Will that be all, sir?" The clerk was in his late teens, maybe Navajo, and had a slow way of working and a big, innocent smile.

"Yeah."

"That'll be two-oh-seven."

Dave handed the kid a five. Then, just to cover his tracks, he pulled out the picture he had of Michael Wright. The kid shook his head.

"How about this guy?" He showed the boy Bobby Earl Bunton's picture next. The clerk leaned forward. Dave let him check it carefully.

"Yes, sir." The clerk thrilled Dave with his answer. "A guy who looked a lot like this came in here in the last hour or so."

"Did you see which way he went?"

"No, sir, but I expect they were heading for the interstate.

"Very likely."

"You a cop?"

"Private investigator."

The kid whistled. "Cool. Bet that's exciting, huh? You after this guy?"

"Could be. Did you happen to notice what kind of car the guy was in and if there was anybody with him?"

The kid thought for a moment. "Some kind of big old car, maybe? I don't remember. I didn't see nobody else."

"That's good enough, son. Thanks a lot." Dave started for the door.

"Hey, mister, wait a minute," the clerk called after him. Dave stopped halfway through the door. "You forgot your change."

Dave waved an index finger at the boy. "Keep it, son."

"Wow." The boy pocketed the nearly three dollar tip from a two dollar plus sale. "Hot diggity damn."

"THIS JUNK HEAP Nesto swapped us don't get five miles to the gallon." Bobby Earl complained after he had Mary Beth stop at a convenience store in Hatch to get gas, a hot burrito, an Orange Slice, and more pecan twirls to fill the boy's apparently limitless desire for junk food. Afterward he had directed her to head for the interstate.

They crossed the bridge over the Rio Grande just out of Hatch, paused at the stop sign at the head of the ramp leading to I-25, and then sped north toward Albuquerque.

"Honey." Mary Beth acted sweet and deferential when they were out on the highway. "Ain't this interstate gonna be crawlin' with police lookin' for y… *us?*"

"Just do what I tell ya. We'll be all right."

"Okay," Mary Beth responded, but Michael nodded his assent,

too. With a disgusted look, Bobby Earl turned away from them both and began staring out the car window.

Miraculously, it seemed to Michael, they drove for nearly an hour without seeing a police car on either side of the highway. He had even begun to settle into an almost calm, road trip frame of mind. But when they were just past Truth or Consequences, Bobby Earl suddenly broke that illusion.

"Take this exit," he yelled without warning, nearly bringing Michael and Mary Beth up off their seats. "Now. Take this one, now."

Mary Beth swerved off the interstate and onto the exit. Michael managed to read something about Elephant Butte Lake as they slid up to the stop sign at the end of the exit. Over to his right he saw a wide, long lake beneath a massive, rocky plateau. *Appropriately named*, he noted.

"Where to, baby?"

"Just a minute." Bobby Earl held up his hand.

Michael looked back toward the highway. Sure enough, right on cue, a highway patrol car zoomed by.

Bobby Earl laughed. "Take a right. I seen a sign for a campground over here somewhere. This is a good time to hole up. They'll be running around like chickens with their heads cut off looking for us, and we'll be nowhere. Right here."

DAVE BISHOP DROVE all the way back to Truth or Consequences and stopped at the same motel he had the night before. He had taken a few exits off I-25, checking out some back roads he thought Bobby Earl Bunton might have used to elude the police, but came up with nothing. By the time he finished checking back into the motel and grabbing something quick to eat, it was late in the short winter day.

With the sun setting so early these days—it was like dusk had begun in mid-afternoon, what with the small mountains to the west blocking the last of the day's light—Dave decided he would have better luck waiting for the fugitives to reemerge the next morning. He flipped on the TV set in his room, sipped from a bottle of beer he'd bought, and gave Ralph another call. Still nothing new. Then he called his mother.

"Where are you, David?"

"Down in Truth or Consequences, Mom."

"What's the weather like?"

"About the same, it's cool. Nice."

"That's nice. Did you take a jacket?"

"Yes, Mother."

Several years ago, after his father had died prematurely, Dave had moved his mother out to Albuquerque to be near him. She had her own place and her own life, just as Dave had his, but they saw each other frequently and acted as occasional support for one another, him mostly economic, she mostly emotional. And, like all mothers, Mrs. Bishop fussed over her boy and was always fretting about him and trying to match him off to this woman or that.

"Are you alone?"

"Of course."

"You spend too much time alone. You're always off somewhere doing something by yourself."

"You know, Mom, you can be as lonely in the middle of half a million people as you can in the middle of an empty desert."

"What in the world is that supposed to mean?"

"I don't know. It just came out."

"You need a wife. Someone like Carol. She's an angel."

"Not that again, Mom. And besides, Carol is happily married."

"Well, someone like her."

"Anyway." Dave tried to redirect the conversation. "Tell Carol thanks for taking you shopping."

"I will. Now, David, you are going to be home for Christmas?"

"No problem, I'll be back in a day or two, max."

"Promise?"

"Promise."

"All right, honey. I better run. I got supper on."

"Okay, Mom, see you soon."

"Be careful, sweetheart."

"Always."

"Bye, bye."

"Bye."

Dave sat the phone down. He had a little bit of a headache from driving back and forth and trying to figure out what this Bunton kid was up to. The inside of his head felt a little mushy, fuzzy, and gray. What was he expending so much effort for? The cops would get the punk soon enough. The kid was too stupid or too belligerent or something to make a quiet getaway somewhere.

It was Wright—*Wyche*—he wanted. And to see if there was a woman. Hell, there had to be, he'd seen her driving. Bunton's moll, he supposed. Though the face he'd seen in that crappy old car hardly had the appearance of a tough criminal. You never knew, though.

As for Wyche, though, the circle had come full round on him. There was some kind of cause and effect at work in the world—maybe. Maybe we do pay for our prior sins. Dave wasn't sure about all that stuff. Philosophy wasn't his long suit.

One thing he was sure about, though. He was very close to Bunton and Wyche. He could feel it. They were nearby, and the whole little scene was going to play itself out to whatever conclusion fate, Bobby Earl Bunton, and the New Mexican authorities might put together. And it was coming down soon.

BOBBY EARL FOUND an isolated spot alongside the lake, and he had Mary Beth pay the camping fee up at the combination convenience store and rental office. He also had her get more junk food, sodas, and ice. When she got back from the long walk, it was dark except for a weak electric light mounted on a thin post at the campsite. He stood beside Michael who sat, still bound hand and foot, at a picnic table underneath the light.

"I want me some food, and then I want some more poon, girl," Bobby Earl told Mary Beth.

"What about Michael?"

"What about Michael?" Bobby Earl mocked her. "Screw him."

"Please, Bobby, I'm tired from drivin'."

"You ain't none such," Bobby Earl snapped. "Now help me put your lover boy wannabe in the trunk."

"No, no." Michael groaned. "Don't put me in there."

"You wanna stay in the car with us and watch us do it, don't you, you sick bastard? I guess you'd like that?"

"No, it's…."

"Bobby, please, cain't we just sit here quiet for a while and eat our food?"

"I guess you wanna be with your new boyfriend, huh?"

"He's not my boyfriend, Bobby, you are. And we all need to eat."

"What were you all talkin' about today when I was asleep in the car?"

"Nothin', Bobby, honey."

"What was it, 'Professor?'" Bobby Earl feigned a punch at Michael. Surprisingly, Michael didn't flinch.

"We didn't talk about anything. She's telling you the truth."

"Shee-it, no way a woman ever tells a man the truth."

"She does," Michael dared say.

"Haw. I reckon you know her so well now."

"No, I…."

"Gimme some food." Bobby Earl switched to Mary Beth, apparently bored with Michael. "You all just talk too much."

Mary Beth handed over a sandwich and an Orange Slice. She gave Michael a quick glance. He shrugged his shoulders. Bobby Earl turned his back on both of them and tore into his food. The boy ate like he was afraid there was somebody standing over his shoulder getting ready to steal it from him. Given the imagined picture Michael had of where this boy had come from and how he had gotten to be the way he was, there probably had been somebody standing over the kid's shoulder—standing there every day of Bobby Earl Bunton's miserable young life.

16

AFTER THE EVENING meal, Bobby Earl put Michael in the trunk of the Buick—over Mary Beth's objections and Michael's spirited if feeble resistance. The door clicked shut over Michael, and he found himself in complete, bound, claustrophobic darkness. His pulse and heart pounded so that he felt them in his eyes, in his ears. For perhaps ten minutes he existed in total, myopic, paralyzed fear.

Then he saw some light filtering through minute cracks in the trunk lid and on the sides near the back of the wheel wells. He felt a tiny stream of cool fresh air. He could breathe, he could see just a little bit. His pulse rate slowly decreased, his heart stopped pounding, he listened to the night. He could hear birds or bats flit by occasionally, and once he heard a car on a road somewhere far to his left.

Twice during his lonely hours in the trunk he heard Mary Beth's muffled cries and felt the shaking of the big vehicle as Bobby Earl took the girl at his pleasure. The rest of the time all was quiet, and as the night wore on Michael relaxed to a degree—not enough to really sleep, but enough to slide into that half-waking, half-dreaming state where stray thoughts play unbidden in the semi-conscious mind.

He thought of the girl and their talk about the miracle of birth. His mind argued to an image of the girl. There is nothing special about birth. Cockroaches and African skinless moles give birth. Everything alive has been born, grows, then dies. The only miracle of life is its mystery. Being. Existence. That's the miracle and the mystery. Why is there anything? Why not nothing? And sad as it made Michael feel in his current predicament, it was true that the external world would little know or care when he, we—all of us—were gone.

His own path, he saw all too well, ended with him, with the end of his life. There would be no children left to the world. No legacy. His was an evolutionary dead end. Death and unremembrance, an inescapable fact. And he saw that he had spent the years of his life as if they were cheap currency, virtually limitless—like an Italian Lira of the soul. He realized then, too, that he had never understood life, the things that went on outside of himself. He neither understood people, nor events—certainly not the world itself. Existence was always the ultimate mystery.

When he was young, he had tried to understand, to engage, to participate. But those revolutionary days were long gone. Revolution? He laughed to himself at his own silliness. There hadn't been a revolution. He hadn't been a revolutionary. He hadn't even been a radical. He had done some things, said some things that were perhaps radical to others. Now he was just a burnout, a shell of who he was or might have been, but he had never bought into the mainstream BS, either. No, that wasn't going to happen.

He was a merely a dissident. An *apostate,* as someone had once called him. Whatever or whoever he was, he would not, could not, follow the "correct" path. Maybe he and his generation were just spoiled kids. Or maladjusted.

Maybe we'd been right, too, he thought. *Maybe.*

Like most older people, at some stage, all you had left of this—your *life*—was memory. You wanted to hope, to look forward to something, but there was nothing else left up the road. You needn't feel sorry about it, nor mourn it. It's just the way it is. Whatever force was out there, whatever power lay behind it, was neither malignant nor benign, it simply was.

When you were in tune with the laws of this force, its harmony, that was good luck, happiness. The opposite brought bad luck, sorrow. But these were all ways of describing subjective states, human conditions unrelated to the great indifference. You were no more than a tiny piece of a huge, unfathomable mystery. But you were no less, either.

He closed his eyes, seeing, feeling, absorbing the darkness. And the darkness was simple and reassuring. He felt calm, almost relaxed. A feeling of release swept over him. He felt at peace with himself, with the big thing out there, whatever it was. He had made his accommodation with it. He sighed and opened his eyes in the darkness. Just then he heard a key go into the trunk lock, and the lid popped open.

"Okay, shitface." Bobby Earl's mouth was twisted into a snarling, malignant smile. "Out of the hole."

Michael tried to climb out, but with his hands and feet bound and his body stiff from being cramped in the trunk, he struggled to get to his knees. Impatiently, Bobby Earl reached inside the trunk and drug him out. Michael banged his shins on the huge rear bumper and fell to the ground in a heap. The boy jerked him to his feet. Michael leaned against the car and groaned. Between his aching shins, the bump on the side of his head, and the bruises and scratches on his body and face, he figured he fit the profile of a kidnap victim. The only positive thing was that the cord around his ankles had come loose. Bobby Earl hadn't noticed.

"Oh, God." Mary Beth, suddenly materialized, breathlessly, between the two men. "Here comes someone. Oh, dear God, it's the police."

"This is your fault, butthead." Bobby Earl turned on Michael. "I oughta waste you right now."

"What'll we do, Bobby?" Mary Beth cried.

"Just shut up and let me handle it."

"Maybe we can outrun him? This car's big and fast."

"Too late." Bobby Earl handed her the .38, holding it low and behind his back. "Here, take this."

"I don't want that."

"Take it and keep it on, dumbass. Get behind him and let me

do the talkin'. You say a word, you punk bastard," he threatened Michael, "and I'll kill you and the lousy cop and ever'body else. You understand me?"

Michael nodded. Mary Beth took the .38 and stood behind Michael, but she didn't hold the weapon on him. Instead of metal at his back, Michael felt the girl hook the shaking fingers of her free hand around his belt loops and hold on tight. In any other situation, it would have felt like a gesture of affection.

"Just be cool," Bobby Earl hissed. "This guy's nothin' but a county mountie."

"Good morning." The deputy sheriff stopped his Jeep near the Buick. "How are you folks doing?"

"We're all right." Bobby Earl nervously eyed Michael and Mary Beth. The deputy kept smiling and slowly got out of his vehicle.

"It's a real pretty place to camp here, along the lake, isn't it?" Bobby Earl backed up a couple of steps.

"Sure is." Mary Beth smiled. She could feel Michael tensing and straining away from her grip on his belt.

"Where you folks from?" The Deputy was still smiling, but his right hand was near his holstered weapon.

"Tucson...." Mary Beth blurted out at the same time Bobby Earl said Deming.

The deputy cocked his head. Bobby Earl eased Nesto's .357 out of the back of his pants.

"Which is it?" The deputy's smile faded.

"Tucson," Mary Beth repeated. Bobby Earl gave her a harsh look.

"I'm from Deming," he told the deputy. "She's from Tucson."

"Oh, I see."

"We're just travelin' around," Mary Beth explained. "Goin' to visit family. Holidays and all, you know."

"Yes, ma'am." The deputy gave the Buick a once over, checking the license plate, looking inside the rolled down windows. "I don't mean to trouble you, but do you mind showing me your registration and proof of insurance. And driver's license, please."

"Oh, gosh." Mary Beth improvised. "We just got the car, and I don't know if we have all that."

"If you purchased the car in this state, ma'am, you've got to have all those things."

"We ain't got 'em." Bobby Earl took a step toward the deputy sheriff. Michael saw the boy's thumb on the hammer of the pistol. He saw what was getting ready to happen.

"Watch out," he yelled at the deputy. "He's got a gun."

Backing away from the car and simultaneously unsnapping the strap on his pistol holster, the deputy tried to draw down on Bobby Earl, but the boy had the element of surprise.

"You son of a bitch," Bobby Earl yelled, bringing the .357 around and firing it nearly point blank at the deputy.

There was a booming discharge. Mary Beth and Michael ducked behind the Buick. The round hit the deputy square in the chest, knocking him backward and down. Bravely, he fought to rise again and lifted his own weapon to fire. But a second round from the .357 hit him in the face, killing him instantly. In that last moment of life, he had pulled the trigger of his own weapon, but the shot was wild, slamming into the back driver's side of his Jeep. Bobby Earl stood over the dead deputy, pointing the pistol at his lifeless, bleeding body, cursing like a mad man.

"Oh, sweet, Jesus," Mary Beth cried, racing from behind the Buick. "Dear God, Bobby Earl. What have you done?"

"Kilt the dumb ass, that's what."

The girl dropped to her knees by the fallen officer, wailing uncontrollably. From behind the Buick, Michael made a run for it. Pushing off the vehicle, he bolted toward the road beyond their campsite. He didn't make ten feet when the explosive roar of the .357 and the whizzing of a deadly round missing his head by inches once again brought him to an instant halt.

In seconds, Bobby Earl was on him, kicking him, shoving him, knocking him to the ground.

"Where you goin', you stupid bastard?"

"Don't hit me." Michael covered his head from the boy's blows. "Please, don't hurt me. Stop."

"Get up, you piece of shit." Bobby Earl grabbed Michael by the shirt and pulled him to his feet. "I ought to clean your ugly ass."

"Stop it." Mary Beth appeared behind the boy. She held the .38 Bobby Earl had given her behind her back. "Leave him alone."

Bobby Earl turned toward her, pulling Michael around with him. "Worried about your little lover boy, are you?"

"You killed that policeman."

"Screw him."

"We'll never get home now. Don't you see what you done?"

"I don't give a damn what I done."

"Please."

"Please what?"

"We gotta give up now. What about my Marcie Kay?"

"Why don't you shut up about that kid? It's all you ever talk about."

"Bobby, don't say that." Mary Beth cried then, cried real tears. "Oh, God, please."

"Shut your hole, woman." The boy pushed Michael toward the door of the Buick. "Now get in and drive. I got to think about what I'm going to do next."

"*Please* don't shoot anybody else, Bobby." Mary Beth sobbed.

"Shut up"—He squeezed Michael and then himself into the back seat behind the narrow space afforded by pushing the front seat forward—"and drive. I don't care who else I shoot now. Just get us the hell out of here."

17

DAVE BISHOP WOKE to a keen sense of anticipation. This would be the day. He could feel it. This Bunton boy didn't have the discipline to keep out of sight for long. He would have to do something to give himself away. His kind of miscreant always did. The boy was too stupid or too thrill happy or too much at war with society to simply steal a car and vanish. No, he had to make a spectacle of it.

Dave just hoped the kid wouldn't get too desperate with the pressure of the police manhunt that was undoubtedly closing in on him at this very moment. Hopefully he wouldn't lose it, go over the top, but you never knew. Up to now, Bobby Earl Bunton had just been another in the seemingly endless parade of modern day, small time hoods and punks. Robbing, stealing, but nothing horrible—yet.

After showering, Dave dressed and prepared to find a good hearty breakfast. Just as he was walking toward the motel door, Ralph called from Albuquerque. The Bunton boy had created his spectacle.

THEY WERE ALMOST to Socorro when Bobby Earl ordered Mary Beth to take the next exit.

"Where are we goin'? Tears ran down the girl's long, thin cheeks.

She had been crying steadily since the boy shot the deputy sheriff. Michael was silent. He had reconciled himself to his own imminent death. Bobby Earl was completely out of control now. There was no telling what he was going to do.

"Take a left," he told Mary Beth when she halted the Buick at the exit stop sign.

She made the turn, crossed over the interstate, and followed the road as it ran in a generally east-west angle toward Socorro. A couple of miles past the interstate, they neared a dirt road that ran southerly off the paved road. Bobby Earl directed her to take it. About a half mile down the road, he ordered her to stop the car.

"Why are we stoppin' here?"

"Get out." Bobby Earl grabbed Michael by the collar and drug him stumbling and falling out of the car onto the road. "Stand up."

"What are you doing, Bobby Earl?" Mary Beth tried to insert herself between the boy and Michael.

"Stay out of it."

"Don't do it. We can still get home. Please don't do anything else."

"Back." Bobby Earl pushed her away.

"Oh, Bobby, honey, *please.*"

"It has to be this way." The boy brandished the .357. "It's too late. This idiot ruined everything."

"No, Bobby. Don't."

"It's too late. He messed it up."

"He didn't do anything."

"Him and all the buttholes like him."

"No, Bobby."

"Stay out of it. It ain't got nothin' to do with you."

"Don't do this."

"Go to hell."

The boy raised the .357 and aimed it directly at Michael's forehead. Michael closed his eyes, tried to control his shaking knees, tried to think of what he should think of at the end. He tried to picture Barbara, his students, Tucson. He couldn't. No images came. No thoughts about life, the world, his own miserable existence. No thoughts—none, neither profound nor mundane. He closed his eyes more tightly and only hoped death would not hurt. And then he heard the tremendous roar of a pistol being fired. But he didn't feel anything hit him. He waited for the impact, waited for the last blackness, the end. He waited.

Nothing happened.

Then he heard the girl sobbing and opened his eyes. Bobby Earl was sprawled on his back in the middle of the recently-graded road, the .357 lying near his lifeless right hand, blood oozing from the socket where his left eye had been. The girl, disconsolate, chest wracked with heaving sobs, was on her knees by the dead boy. She moaned and cried, calling out the boy's name.

When Michael had regained enough of his senses to realize he was safe, alive, and now out of danger for the first time in nearly forty-eight hours, he went to the girl and knelt by her side.

"You saved my life, Mary Beth." He put his hands on the girl's shaking shoulders. "You saved your life."

"I… I killed him. I shot Bobby Earl."

Michael ran a bound hand through the girl's hair and rubbed tears off her cheek. "He would have killed us both. Me. You. He lost it. He was crazy."

"Now I'll never see my baby again." Mary Beth's voice quaked with emotion.

"Yes, you will." Michael assured her. "Yes, you will. I swear to you, you will."

"Oh, God." The girl broke down again. "Oh, Lord. I just want to see my baby again."

"Where's the gun, Mary Beth?" The girl cried all the more. Michael saw the .38 in the dirt by her right foot. He reached over and picked it up. "C'mon." He helped her to her feet. "We've got to get you out of here."

Though the inconsolable girl was virtually limp, nearly dead weight, Michael managed to get her seated in the rider's side of the Buick. He then wrestled with the cords on his wrists until his hands were free again at last. Then he went to the back of the car and opened the trunk. There was an old shirt of Bobby Earl's there, and Michael used it to wipe the girl's prints off the pistol as best he could.

Next he gripped the pistol as if he were going to fire it and then held it by the cylinder and the barrel with both of his hands. He then walked back up beside the girl who sat with her head in her hands. At least her body had stopped shaking.

"Cover your ears, Mary Beth." The girl was red-eyed, not understanding. "I'm just going to shoot this gun into the ground."

She covered her ears and lowered her head to her lap. Michael walked over by the body of Bobby Earl. He aimed the .38 at a ditch across the road and pulled the trigger. When the pistol went off, Mary Beth jumped. Michael almost dropped the weapon, grabbed it gingerly by the handle, tossed it beside Bobby Earl.

"Okay." He climbed into the Buick and started it up. "Let's get the hell out of here."

AFTER SPENDING THE better part of the morning on an unsuccessful reconnoitering of every county and back road he could find in the general area of Elephant Butte Lake, Dave Bishop gave up his fruitless search and headed back up I-25. He couldn't believe how near he must be or have been to the fugitives and how close by the shooting of the deputy sheriff had been. And he had definitely passed them yesterday out on the Hatch-Deming highway. He was sure of that now. And yet they were still at large. The police hadn't caught them. He hadn't caught them.

He was like a floating tracking mechanism, sort of accurate but not nearly enough so. He had had this one pegged early, but, he realized, he might not be the one to complete it. Having a good idea about something was not the same as accomplishing it.

You had to have closure to get paid. And closing was definitely not the same as finishing. Not to the agencies who forked over the cash for the type of bounty hunting he was trying to pull off here. In the midst of his self-evaluation, Dave passed Socorro and was fifteen or so miles north of the little desert town when he got Ralph's second call.

"Bunton is dead? And Wright's in custody in Socorro? Son of a gun."

"That's the skinny," Ralph confirmed. *"Wright just came in by himself. Not long ago, either. This is hot off the presses. Got it straight from one of my old partners in the Socorro PD."*

"The punk is dead?"

"As a doornail."

"I'll be. And the girl?"

"There's nothing about a girl."

"No girl? At all? Even after those earlier reports?"

"That's what this Wright character said," Ralph explained. Dave saw an exit coming up and took it.

"Okay, Ralphie, I'm going in to check it out."

"To Socorro?"

"Right."

"Want me to come down?"

"No, I screwed this one up for us money-wise, but I want to check out the Wright guy, anyway."

Dave crossed over the interstate and took the exit back south toward Socorro. As he pulled back onto the highway, a regional bus roared by on the other side of the highway heading north. It belched black smoke as it rumbled on toward Albuquerque.

"See you when you get back," Ralph said. *"Don't worry about the money. We got more deadbeat perps than we can shake a stick at."*

"Okay. Would you have Carol call my mother again? Tell her I'll be home late tonight sometime."

"Will do, bud. Talk to you later."

"Later." Dave ended the call and drove on to Socorro.

"YOU'RE IN LUCK," the clerk at the combination convenience store and bus depot told Michael. "There's one due not too long from now. Going to Albuquerque."

"I'll take it." Michael pulled out a wad of Bobby Earl's left over cash—most, if not all, of it his own, anyway. It still gave him an odd feeling of using stolen money.

"One adult?" The clerk looked at Mary Beth, who stood behind Michael, head down, staring at the dirty floor.

"Just one."

"Very good." The clerk handed Michael the ticket.

"Thanks."

"Thank you, sir."

Michael turned to Mary Beth. She didn't look up right away. He glanced back at the clerk, and the young man busied himself with other work. Michael then handed the ticket and the rest of the money he had to Mary Beth. When she raised her head, her eyes were filled with tears.

"It'll be all right." He patted her hand and led her away from the counter. She fought back a sob. "It's okay."

"No, it's not. I ki—"

"Shh." Michael quieted her, taking her hands in his briefly. "You saved us both. You didn't do anything wrong. You're a good person." She began to cry again.

"C'mon." He touched her cheek and lightly ran his hand through her soft, fine hair. "I'll take care of this. Nobody has to know you were ever even here." She leaned her head against his shoulder. He kissed the top of her head. "We're going to get you back to your baby."

"I miss her so much."

"I know you do."

Mary Beth dabbed at the tears running down her face with a Kleenex she found in her purse. She tried to smile for Michael, then leaned over and kissed him on the cheek.

"Thank you."

"We need to get you some snacks for the trip."

Michael guided the girl down an aisle and out of view of the clerk and a couple of customers by the counter. When they had gotten her a nice little stash of treats, they returned to the front. Mary Beth paid, managing a smile for the young clerk.

"Let's find someplace outside to wait." Michael took her arm, and they walked to the front door.

"All right."

THE CLERK'S ESTIMATE of the bus arriving "not too long from now" proved to be a poor one indeed. The better part of an agonizingly slow hour passed for Michael and Mary Beth before the belching, wheezing TNM&O bus finally pulled up to the convenience store.

"Thank God." Michael sighed deeply. "Here's the bus."

"I feel so tired." Mary Beth essayed a smile.

"I know you do." Michael again ran his hand through the girl's hair. She briefly touched his hand with her own. "Here." He took her paper sack of travel treats.

Holding the sack in his right hand, he put his left hand around Mary Beth's waist and helped her over to the bus. A couple of people got off, and then the driver came out to unload some packages from the cargo hold underneath the bus. Three people lined up to board, and Michael drew Mary Beth to one side.

"Listen." He handed her the sack. "Don't go straight home. Wait a few days somewhere. You have people in Fort uh...."

"Smith. Fort Smith."

"Yes, Fort Smith. But don't go there right away. Don't go straight home yet."

"I have an aunt up in Missouri, up around Joplin."

"Good, go there. When you get to Albuquerque, buy a ticket for Joplin. You can do that, right?"

"Yes. I'm used to buses."

"Okay."

The bus driver closed up the hold and began boarding the other passengers. Michael held Mary Beth's arm as they walked to the bus door. She gave the driver her ticket and then threw her arms around Michael's neck.

"Thank you. I'll never forget you."

"Go on. Live a good life with your little girl." Mary Beth leaned back, and Michael saw the tears in her eyes again. "Go on."

"Miss." The driver indicated the steps leading up into the bus. "You can get on now."

"Goodbye." Mary Beth slowly let go of Michael. "Thank you."

"Goodbye. Everything will be okay."

"I'll take care of her for you, sir." The driver helped Mary Beth board the bus. "She's in good hands."

With a wave, the driver climbed into the bus and shut the door. Michael stepped back a few feet and tried to spot Mary Beth, but the windows were too darkly tinted to see well into the vehicle. With a smoke-belching roar, the bus unceremoniously pulled out and rumbled away from the station leaving Michael standing there alone. When it had disappeared from sight, he calmly went back into the convenience store to ask directions to the Socorro police station.

18

SITTING QUIETLY BY himself in the Socorro police station, Michael's headache was gone for the first time in months. His mind was as close to clear as he could remember it having been of late. He rested his head in his hands, waiting for the FBI, the New Mexico and Arizona state police, the local and national media, whoever might still be coming to grill him—when a man suddenly appeared at his side.

"Mind if I sit here?" Michael didn't answer, but he scooted a little to his left on the bench. The man sat down. "Merry Christmas."

Michael took a little start. He had completely forgotten what time of year it was, much less that it was the holiday season.

"Yeah." He didn't look at the man. "Merry Christmas."

"Not a good time to be sitting alone in a police station in the middle of nowhere. Assuming you *are* alone." Michael chanced a quick peek at the guy. Probably another cop. "You alone?"

Michael fidgeted in his seat and began to wonder what this guy's game was.

There was a long pause. Then the man spoke again, crisply, bluntly. "Where's the girl, Michael?"

Michael fought an impulse to jump up and run away. "W—what girl? And how do you know who I am?"

"One topic at a time."

"Who are you?" Michael considered the guy. There was something vaguely familiar about him.

"You're going to say there wasn't a woman?"

"There wasn't."

"No?"

"No."

"Come on, now, witnesses say there was a girl."

"No."

"So it was just you and…."

"Bobby Earl."

"Ah, yes, Mister Bunton. Got to know Bobby Earl pretty well, did we?"

"What do you think?" Michael was defiant. He was getting tired of this guy and his questions already.

"I think you're protecting somebody, a girl actually. Whoever she was. It probably won't take much to find out, you know."

Michael didn't react.

"It's not like anyone blames you for what you did or say you did. Bunton was a useless piece of shit, and he got what he deserved. Although I did lose some money on the deal. And a couple of days work."

"I've already explained to the sergeant here what happened. It was just me and Bobby Earl. And a couple of his ex-con buddies over in Deming. I don't even remember their names."

"You're awfully good at keeping stuff to yourself, aren't you, buddy? Always were."

"You're not one of these cops. Who are you?' Michael demanded.

The man smiled. "Whenever I think of you, I can't help but remember some of those lines from an old Dylan song you used to quote all the time. You remember, something about Fidel Castro and his beard."

Michael's brow furrowed. Images from a distant past played at the corners of his mind, recollections—it felt—from another lifetime. The Dylan song the man referred to popped into his head—along with another memory. He really studied the man this time, carefully. He sucked in his breath like he'd been hit squarely in the solar plexus.

"Bishop. Dave Bishop. My God."

"Relax. I haven't blown your cover. Which is more than I can say for you and your hippie friends."

"That was… was decades ago. How… *why?*"

"Coincidence, Michael. Chance. Fate. Luck. Karma. You pick it."

"So you got me at last. Big Deal. Does it matter anymore?"

"You tell me, pal. You're the one's been underground all this time. The eternal revolutionary. Last of the old radical hippies."

"Not exactly."

"What did you hippies think was going to happen back then with your revolution, anyway?"

"We didn't call ourselves hippies. People like you did. We were just freaks to ourselves."

"Oh, yeah, excuse me. What did you 'freaks' think was going to happen? It was going to be all peace, love, sex, dope? And rock and roll?"

"I don't know what we thought. It doesn't matter now, does it? That time's long gone. Gone forever."

"Dumped on the ash heap of history."

"Under the dung hill of triumphant capitalism," Michael retorted.

"Once a commie, always one, eh?"

"Hardly." Michael almost smiled.

"Was it you turned me in back then, Michael. Back there in Columbia? When you were still Michael Wyche? Before you slipped into Mexico on me?"

"No, it wasn't me." Bishop was quiet. "Are you going to turn me?"

They sized each other up.

"Frankly, Michael, I don't know what went on out there in the desert, and I don't really care. The world isn't going to miss another Bobby Earl Bunton more or less. Hell, you probably did us all a service. Maybe even squared your karma some."

"You're not going to tell them who I am?"

"No, I won't tell them. I'd rather have you out here in the cold where you've been since I last saw you. After all this time, still on the outside looking in."

"Maybe for the first time in my life I've done something that puts me on the inside, you know?"

"All this for some PWT girl?" Michael was silent. "Well, it doesn't matter to me if you shot the guy or she did. I've found you at last. You didn't get away."

"I don't understand. If it meant so much to you, why aren't you going rat me out?"

"First of all, it's not my call anymore. And besides, looking at you now, I can see it's all over. Whatever gesture you're making here is too little and too late. You've already gotten your sentence, Michael. It's your life. I sentence you to your own life. You just have to live it out by yourself."

Michael lowered his head and observed the beginnings of wrinkles on the backs of his hands. He thought about Bishop's words. Gave them the importance they deserved.

"Yes, that's exactly right. I do have to live out the rest of my life by myself, on my own. And now I can."

Bishop stared at his ex-prey and saw an unexpected resolve appear there. He formed the first words of another question but was cut off by a sudden bustling at the door of the police station. The doors swung open and a crew of TV people rushed into the room. A pretty young Hispanic woman, obviously the reporter, came over to the two men. She looked them both over, then spoke to Bishop.

"Michael Wright?" Bishop jerked a thumb at Michael, who stood up. "Can we talk to you, sir?" The woman addressed Michael. Bishop was no longer of interest and immediately dropped from her consciousness. "We'd like to ask you about the carjacking."

"Sure." Michael smiled, the hint of what it once meant to be a teacher, perhaps a person of principle, reemerging from the lost place into which it had gone years ago. "I'll be glad to tell you all that's happened to me."

PANHANDLE

Out on the Road

A GUSTING WIND swirled erratically across the empty West Texas fields, lifting and scattering little clouds of dust that rose up behind the heels of Buddy Harris' worn and dirty boots with each step he took over the crumbling, dry land. Wisps of sand hit against the side of his face, and he turned away from time to time to protect his eyes from the fine but sharp-edged topsoil.

Sometimes when the wind kicked up harder, it swept over the thin, barbed wire fences surrounding the dead fields, rattling the twisted metal and slapping scraps of paper and pieces of plastic sacks against rocks and posts in its way. Other times when it blew straight and hard, it whistled—whistled a long, high lonesome sound that reminded Buddy of old Hank Williams songs he'd heard his daddy play years ago.

That wind sound recalled to the boy memories of farther back up in the Panhandle around Amarillo where he'd gone many times with old Luke Miller to sell cattle and horses. The wind blew hard and cold there in the heart of the Panhandle, and it made a man feel as alone as if he were the only person alive in the whole territory—how it must've felt when there were only Indians in the land and trail herders were passing through.

While he walked along, another sound began to work its way into his consciousness. It was a *whooshing* sound, like a ground level wind or shallow water being forded by an old car with slick, bald tires. Looking to his left, out to the two-lane highway beside which he walked, he realized that a car—or truck—was approaching. As the vehicle came toward him from behind, he drew his mind fully back from that distant, silent place it had been and began again to tune into the real world around him.

It was barely gray light, another twenty minutes or so before sunrise, and he was walking by the highway outside of town, barely aware of real time or place. He stopped for a moment to get his bearings, the roar of the vehicle—he could definitely tell it was a truck now—growing louder as it neared him from behind.

He looked up as the pickup shot by him, a clanking dark beast chewing up the stillness of the morning air. There were two young men inside that he recognized, but he was sure that the occupants had not done the same of him as they blew past in the early light of day. Pausing by a fence post, he watched until they rounded a distant corner by a sparse stand of cottonwood trees and disappeared.

"Headin' for the Black Toast," he declared quietly to the empty road and fields.

The thought of the Black Gold Café, its name an anachronism of Seco's faded oil past and rechristened the Black Toast or Caje's by locals accustomed to the commonly burnt breakfast toast, which was about a mile or so on up the road, made Buddy hungry. He was thinking of a plate-size pancake with bacon and eggs, coffee, and that famous Cajun toast, as his old friend Johnny Dupree, the owner of the pickup that had just sped by him, used to call it.

It occurred briefly to Buddy that he could not remember his last meal. For a few tiring moments then, his stomach betrayed him, and he felt as if he would have to stop until the cramping passed. But with the steadily increasing light showing him it was going to be a nice morning, calm and tranquil, he kept at his slow pace, just walking, letting his hunger subside, putting itself back there with all the other things of greater and lesser significance that gnawed frequently, if not always gently, at the edges of his awareness.

About a quarter mile up the road on his right, he saw a grazing field with a handful of cattle munching on ankle-high grass. Across the road to the left and up another eighth of a mile or so was a small farmhouse. *The old Phelps's place*, he thought. *And probably still their cows, too.*

As he neared the farm, a solitary milk cow lowed unhappily at him, and then a big German Shepherd-looking mix of a dog came rushing down the Phelps's long dirt driveway. The dog raced out onto the road barking and baring his teeth, but when Buddy stopped and squared off at it, the animal suddenly halted its charge.

"For cryin' out loud, Buck," he called over at the dog. "Cain't you remember anything? Stop that barkin' right now."

The dog cocked his head to one side and quit barking. Buddy crossed the highway to the dog and slapped his hands together. The dog, slowly remembering, began to move forward again. Then it started barking again, but this time it was a happy yelp of greeting, and the animal jumped all around excitedly. Buddy grabbed the big pooch and rough-housed it, petting the thick-headed creature over and over.

"That's more like it, you old mutt." He rolled the dog over onto its back where it flopped back and forth in the dirt by the road. In the midst of the happy reunion, a man came out of the Phelps's house and called for the dog. Buddy pushed Buck up to his feet and swatted him on the butt.

"You better get your old fanny back home." For a moment, the dog was unsure of his loyalty. "Go on now." Buddy heard someone call from the house.

The dog barked and ran off energetically. Buddy laughed and dusted his hands off on his dirty jeans. He could see what was probably old man Phelps up by the house now, and he made a small wave that was not returned. Shrugging, he smiled to himself and headed on up the road toward the Black Toast.

The Black Toast

AS BUDDY NEARED the café's gravel parking lot, the front door banged open, and a tall, thin, redheaded woman came out. He paused to watch her. It was Suzie Eason, the fast, good-looking wife of Grant Eason, the well-liked history teacher at Seco High. Grant had gone out of his way to help Buddy back in the latter's school days and the younger man never forgot it. Now, he shook his head at the sight of Suzie. She was a nice enough woman, but she had a wandering eye, and everybody knew it. Even, or especially, Grant.

Suzie acted like she was in a big hurry and without even glancing over hopped right into a big, new F-150 pickup. Buddy studied her from where he stood and watched as she cranked up the truck and with a spray of gravel tore out of the café parking lot and shot out onto the highway heading back into town. He turned away and walked on into the Black Toast.

The place smelled great. It was warm and humid inside and made him yawn involuntarily. People were laughing and talking, and the waitresses and cooks barked instructions back and forth to each other.

Del Holland, the long-time owner of the Black Gold Café—he didn't care much for the locals' nickname for his place—had put a down payment on the rundown restaurant with his mustering out pay from the service and through years of hard work and frugal business practices built it into Seco's most successful greasy spoon. It was frequented by working men, farmers, a handful of professional people slumming, high school kids, and that pile of young people you see in most small towns that are not too long out of high school but not headed now, nor ever, to any other institution of learning other than the school of life experience—hard knocks it used to be called.

Del stood behind the cash register just to the left of the front door. He nodded to Buddy as if they had just seen each other yesterday. In return, Buddy touched the brim of his worn Texas Tech baseball cap—the only remaining possession that dated from his last days in Seco.

Looking around the café, he took in the sights and sounds before committing to a place to sit. Some people had stopped talking when he came in and were staring at him, but the majority of the folks just went on about the business of having their breakfasts. The two boys who had roared by him in the yellow pickup were seated to his right a couple of booths up. Seeing an empty stool at the long counter ahead and on the left, Buddy walked toward it.

"What you doin' back here, Harris?" Johnny Dupree drawled as Buddy went by. "We done figured you'd light out for parts far from the Panhandle."

"Everybody's got to be somewhere, Cowboy." Buddy turned casually, matching Johnny's easy smile. They had worked several summers together on local farms and ranches, where Johnny had accrued the nickname "Cowboy" due to his skill with horses. He reached out now and shook Buddy's hand. Buddy tapped his cap to Johnny's companion.

"You remember my cousin Lloyd, don't ya?" Johnny pointed to the younger boy.

"Sure. How you doin', Lloyd?"

"Awhl right."

"Mighty nice of you boys to welcome me home and all."

"How's that?" Johnny asked.

"You danged near run me down out on the road little bit ago," Buddy explained.

"That was you out there on the road?"

"Already forgot all about your old pal, huh?"

"Naw, man, I'm sorry. I didn't recognize you, Buddy. Hell, I'd a stopped if I had."

"It's all right. You was goin' so fast, you'da killed yourselves trying to stop for me." Lloyd snickered.

"Same old Harris." Johnny laughed. "We was goin' so fast, we was practically here before we even realized there'd been somebody out there. You ain't sore, are ya?"

"Naw, I was just kiddin'."

"You back for a while?"

"Cain't say, yet. Just got here."

"Yeah, sure." Johnny took a drink of coffee. "Wanna join us?"

"I'll catch you later, Cowboy. I'm gonna eat at the counter. I'm so hungry it'd scare even you two to watch me hammer this chow."

"Suit yourself. We'll catch you later."

"You boys take it easy." Buddy turned toward the counter. "I'm gonna get me some food. I'm pretty hungry."

"You seen Patsy yet?" Johnny called as Buddy began walking away.

"Just got here."

"How was it up there?" Johnny implied the penitentiary.

"Tell you about it some other time."

"Awhl right."

Buddy parked himself on a stool about midway down the restaurant bar and took off his hat. He dusted it against his jeans and set it over his right knee. When he looked up, Rosa Avila, Del's long time and long-suffering waitress was standing in front of him on the other side of the counter. She smiled sweetly. He smiled back.

Buddy had been gone close to two and a half years, and the time had done nothing for Rosa Avila if not improve what was already a really pretty girl. She had her long black hair done up and pinned behind her head, and her brown eyes sparkled with good will. She was a short girl, with a slight tendency toward thickness, but she was young enough to carry the extra flesh and manage to still be very appealing.

He soaked up her light brown complexion, her firm, full lips, high cheekbones, and pudgy little nose. He let his eyes take in her plump breasts, her mostly flat tummy, her wide hips and thighs and then went back up to her lovely face and those deep, kind, brown eyes.

"What'll it be, mister?" she teased, flattered by his long appraisal of her charms.

"Rosa, whatever your pretty little heart desires."

She giggled. "I mean for breakfast, silly."

"So did I." Buddy grinned.

"Buddy Harris, you ain't changed a bit."

"How could I?"

"Tell me your order, smarty, before Del calls me away."

"Okay, give me some hot coffee, a big mug, with sugar and lots of cream. And one of them big pancakes, a scrambled egg, and some crisp bacon. I'm starvin'."

"You act like you ain't had any good food in a long. . . ." Rosa began. "I'm sorry, Buddy."

"Don't you worry about it none. You didn't do anything wrong."

"I'm sorry. I'll get your order."

"Coffee first, okay?"

"You bet."

"Thanks, beautiful." Buddy winked. Rosa gave him a shyly flirtatious smile and went to place the order.

He was near the end of his second cup of sweet, milky coffee and several bites into his pancakes, egg, and bacon when Sheriff J. T. Emerson made a production of entering the café. Nearly everyone stopped eating and talking—except for Buddy. Sheriff Emerson stood by the register talking to Del Holland for several moments before he noticed Buddy. The minute he did, he stopped talking. Buddy happened to glance over just at that moment, and Emerson made a beeline for him.

"Hell," Buddy muttered. "Cain't even finish one meal."

"Well." Sheriff Emerson came right up beside Buddy. "If it isn't the tough guy."

Sheriff J. T. Emerson was tall and heavy-boned. He stood over six feet in his sheriff's boots and had long ago passed the two hundred pound barrier. He was thirty-eight years old, and some of that weight had shifted downward from his chest to his stomach, but he was still a big, powerful man. He was used to wielding his authority without question although his face showed little of that natural authority. He was weak-eyed and weak-jawed, developing a jowly, cowardly look. All in all, he appeared to be a man hiding his natural insecurity behind a gun and a badge.

"I *said,"* he repeated, when Buddy didn't respond, "if it ain't the tough guy."

"Isn't." Buddy corrected him. "You should say 'isn't,' not 'ain't.'"

"Same smart-mouth Harris. Three years in the pokey and you ain't changed a bit."

"Twenty-eight months." Buddy corrected the lawman again.

"Like I said, smart mouth, smart ass."

Buddy didn't take the bait. He continued eating his breakfast. The restaurant was deathly quiet. No one was making, taking, or getting orders. The place held its collective breath.

"I suppose you came back because of your old maiden aunt." Sheriff Emerson was loud enough for all to hear. "And I'll give you that. It's only right with her passin' and all, but you be quick about takin' care of your business and then be on your way—soon. You're not welcome in Seco, or anywhere in my county."

"Law says I can settle anywhere I please. Long as I sign up with a parole officer."

"I'm tellin' you to move on. Finish your meal and your business in Seco and then find yourself a way out of town. Straight away."

"Mighty neighborly of you." Buddy finished a combined bite of pancake, egg, and bacon. He then took a long drink of coffee before looking over at Sheriff Emerson. "I settle the things I come to settle, then I'll be gone."

"See that you do. And do it fast. Make it quick and clean and legal, or I'll see to it personal that you go straight back to prison. Do I make myself clear?"

"Abundantly."

"Hmph, yardbird talk. I see prison agreed with you."

Buddy took a long drink of coffee and didn't speak. Emerson scowled at him but began to move away. When the sheriff turned his back, Buddy flipped him off. Rosa Avila couldn't restrain a laugh. Emerson growled at her as he stomped back up to the front door.

"Morning, there, Sheriff." Del greeted the lawman as he passed by the register.

"Bull," Emerson groused as he stormed out of the café.

Luke Miller's Place

"OLE J. T. SURE still has a hard-on for you, don't he?" Johnny Dupree steered his battered pickup out onto the highway in front of the Black Gold Café. He and Lloyd were giving Buddy a ride to the only place Buddy could think of where he might stay for a while—old Luke Miller's place.

"I imagine he does."

"You damn near killed that stupid nephew of his," Johnny added. "I mean… I'm sorry, man, I shouldn't have brought that up."

"It's all right, Cowboy. It's the truth."

"Still got a raw deal. Prison and all. Just for kickin' that punk's butt."

"What happened?" Lloyd sat between the older young men. "I just remember you goin' away, Buddy. I was too small to know what was really goin' down."

"Never mind about it," Johnny told his cousin. "It ain't none of our business."

"Ahh, hell. It ain't like it's a big secret or nothin'. Leastwise not here in Seco, anyway."

"I didn't mean no disrespect, Buddy."

"That's okay, kid. I was wrong to whip that boy so bad back then, and it cost me. But I done my time, and now I'm back, and that's all there is to it."

"Was it bad in there, Buddy?"

"Lloyd," Johnny warned, giving the younger boy a harsh look. He turned the pickup off the highway and down a dirt road leading away from town to the southeast.

"I'm sorry."

"It was bad sometimes." Buddy answered the boy's question anyway. "Mostly I was just bored. Twenty-eight months in there will make you stir crazy. I reckon that's where the word comes from."

"I reckon. I ain't never knowed nobody that went to jail that long."

"Make sure you don't, Lloyd. Never go to jail. It ain't worth whatever it was that you so had to do on the outside. Believe me."

"You listen to him, Lloyd. That's a man knows."

"You bet, Johnny. I am listenin'. I understand."

For a few minutes the three young men drove on in silence, then Buddy spoke up. "Oh, man, John. I almost forgot. I was terrible sorry to hear about your dad's passing."

"You knew about it?" Johnny looked over at Buddy.

"Yeah, even in there I got word. I know you two were real close."

"It was like half of me drained out or somethin'."

"How's your sister doin'?"

"Kate? She's doing okay. She has her bad times and some good ones. We're thinkin' of maybe moving over by Albuquerque."

"Cool," Lloyd interjected.

"I got some connections with an auction barn over there." Johnny went on. "They always need riders and wranglers."

"Really?" Buddy scratched his stubbly chin.

"Remind me I'll get you the address and stuff if you want."

"Sounds cool to me." Lloyd tossed in again.

"You're too young." Johnny dismissed his cousin.

"Shoot."

"Maybe I'll take you up on that," Buddy told Johnny.

"Any time."

"I could do it in a year or two." Lloyd insisted.

"Sure you could, Lloyd." Buddy smiled at the kid. "Sure you could."

"There's old Luke's." Johnny brought the long chat to an end. Just up ahead on the left was an old two-story farmhouse.

Buddy took in the house that had practically been his home for the last years of his life leading up to jail. It was mostly the same except for some places needing repair. There were some planks broken on the front steps, the roof could use shingling, and the whole place would look better with a fresh paint job over its currently faded white facade.

Luke was getting a little long in the tooth to keep the place up right. When Buddy was still in high school, his parents died, and the old man took him in like he was his own son. Buddy would never forget that.

"How's he doin' these days, Cowboy?"

"I reckon he's slowed up some from the old days." Johnny pulled into the driveway beside the house. "But he's still Luke Miller. That's better'n most men when they was in their twenties." Buddy laughed.

"There he is." Lloyd motioned toward a tall, slightly hunched over figure at the front screen door of the house.

"Want us to wait for you, Buddy?"

"Naw. I can always stay in the bunkhouse if it ain't got too run down while I been gone. I appreciate you boys givin' me a lift out here."

"All right then, you take it easy. We'll be seein' you around."

"See you fellows around." Buddy climbed out of the pickup.

"So long, Buddy." Lloyd waved.

"Catch you boys later."

Waving at old Luke as they backed out of the driveway, Johnny and Lloyd headed back into town, Johnny's old pickup banging and clanking along the dirt road. At the door of the house, Buddy and Luke faced each other through the screen door.

As a young man, Luke Miller had been every bit as good a horseman as Cowboy Johnny Dupree was now. Luke was tall and strong, always serious and dependable, sometimes rowdy in his youth, mostly kind overall. He had gotten lucky and landed a government contract for beef when he was in his early thirties, and he used that opportunity to expand his small startup ranch into a successful long lasting business.

Over the years he had married, had children, made and lost a pile of money, and found the time to help a few people in need—such as a youthful Buddy Harris. All in all, most folks thought of Luke as a good man, a solid citizen of the closed, somewhat entropic world of Seco, Texas.

Luke's wife had passed when the couple were in their sixties, all but one divorced daughter had moved away from town, and Luke's immediate family now consisted primarily of his granddaughter, Laci Jean, and Pedro, a hired hand, another octogenarian, who had worked for Luke so long—nearly forty years—that he had become as much a part of the family, if not more so, than the seldom-seen offspring and their children.

Now in his early eighties, Luke's once wide shoulders were a little rounded, he was hunched over a bit, and his gait was slow and stiff. Still, even as an aged image of his former self he was well respected by the folks who made up the mixed community of ranchers and oil people that was Seco and its environs.

"Welcome, son." Luke opened the door. "It's been a long time."

"Yes, sir, it has." Buddy allowed, taking off his ballcap as he stepped into the hallway leading to the living room in Luke's house. The two men shook hands formally. Luke was not a man of easy emotion or outward displays of affection.

"Coffee?" The old man took a left turn from the hallway into a small kitchen. Buddy stayed outside by the door.

"Naw, thanks. I just had some down at the Toast."

"Go on and settle in then. Put your stuff up."

"I ain't even got any stuff." Buddy laughed. "Just what I got on me."

"You still got some clothes and boots out in the bunkhouse. You can use those if you ain't outgrowed 'em."

"Sounds good. I appreciate you hangin' on to 'em for me."

"You eat already, too?"

"Yes, sir."

"Well, if you want to rest up a while there in the livin' room, I'm gonna cook a quick breakfast, and then I have to go into town."

"That'd be good. I guess I should go in, too, and check in with somebody so's they know I'm in town."

"Well, this is Saturday, so there's probably nobody around for that sort of thing."

"Oh, yeah. I kind of lost track of time the last few days. Didn't know it was the weekend. I suppose I can check in with whoever anytime I please next week."

"I suppose so."

After Luke had his breakfast, he took Buddy out back of the house by the hay barn. The day was warming up, and chickens scurried around the yard clucking and pecking at stray seeds in the thin grass. A couple of lazy dogs yawned and watched the men languidly.

"Still got Charley and Scooter, I see."

"They ain't worth the food I put in their fat bellies." Luke laughed.

"Hey, you old mutts," Buddy called to the dogs. They stirred slightly but were content just to let Buddy come over and pat them both on the head.

"Got a surprise for you." Luke opened the front of the barn. Inside was Buddy's old Chevy pickup, looking exactly like it had when the boy went away.

"Well, I'll be darned. You kept the dang thing."

"Runnin', too."

"Son of a gun."

"Go on, give 'er a try."

Buddy opened the door and hopped behind the wheel. Sure enough, it only took a couple of cranks on the starter to bring the pickup back to life.

"Sweet."

"I imagined you'd need that when you came home."

"I can't thank you enough, Luke."

"Ain't nothin' but an old pickup."

"Still, I…."

"I gotta run into town for some things." Luke deflected Buddy's thanks. "I 'spect you have some people to get reacquainted with."

"I do. And I thank you truly, sir."

"I know you do, boy. You were always good about that. Pickup'll give you more freedom than taggin' along with me, anyway."

"Yes, sir, it will. Although I never minded taggin' along with you."

"Well, you feel free to come and go as you please. The bunkhouse is always open to you."

"Thanks a bunch, I really do appreciate it."

Going Into Town

WHEN BUDDY WENT back into town, about mid-day, he found several of his old friends exactly where he figured they might be, eating hamburgers and shooting eight ball at Chino's Pool Hall on Main Street. For decades, the young boys of Seco had hung out at Chino's, learning to shoot pool, talking about girls and work, eating the greasy hamburgers and French fries that Chino cooked up in his smelly, dirty little kitchen off to one side of the pool table area.

Chino had three tables. Pretty good ones for a crappy little place like his was. He also had a couple of pinball machines in one corner and a few barstools near the window to the kitchen where the food was dispensed to the usual crowd of late year high schoolers, farmhands, and other local day workers.

Chino himself, a Mexican-American the origin of whose name no one actually knew, was getting old now, maybe in his mid-sixties was a best guess by his clientele. His establishment, because of beer on the premises where underage boys shot pool, was barely legal, but the local police had left him alone forever. Perhaps, it was rumored, because they got a cut of his considerable daily take.

When Buddy walked into Chino's around noon, there were maybe ten, twelve people in the place. Most sat on the barstools or stood around the kitchen window, eating the ubiquitous burger and fries.

At one pool table, he saw Johnny Dupree and Art Price, another of his old friends.

Among the eaters were Gordon Carver, a camo-fatigued Viet Nam veteran rumored to be suffering from PTSD, and Clu Tucker, a thirty-five-ish oilfield worker, roustabout, and well-known womanizer. If the woman was from Seco, Clu had either had her or made a try for her.

"Well, look what the cat drug in." Clu laughed, looking up as Buddy walked into the pool hall. "You can't tell who they'll let out of the slammer these days."

"What do you say, Clu?" Buddy smiled.

He had already determined not to take offense or react to any jokes or baiting about his recent accommodations. He would act like he had been working out of state. That was all.

"Hey, Buddy." Gordon shook his hand.

"How are you, Gordon?"

"I been better."

"Ain't we all."

"Didn't know you'd be comin' back here."

"Gotta get a few things sorted out, Clu."

"No doubt."

"Hey, Buddy." Cowboy was at a pool table, and he paused in his eight-ball game with Art Price. "Grab a cue. Play the winner."

"Hey, dude," Art called over.

"Hey, Artie," Buddy called back. "See ya fellows." He pointed at Clu and Gordon.

"See ya." They turned back to their food.

Buddy went to a rack of cues mounted on a nearby wall and selected a medium-weight one. He sighted down it and then rolled it on an empty table to see if it was too warped—even by Chino's standards.

"Won't do you no good to try and find a good cue in here." Cowboy laughed when Buddy got up alongside him and Art.

"Gotta act like it, though." Buddy smiled.

"Same old Buddy." Art playfully tapped his old friend on the shoulder. He'd never known anyone who had been sent to prison before, and he was a little unsure of picking back up where he and Buddy had left off as good high school pals.

"Same old. Which one of you losers am I gonna whip next?"

After the boys had played a handful of games, Chino's began to empty out, the workers heading back to the rest of their day's work. Reluctantly, Cowboy also had to go, and so he said his goodbyes and left Buddy alone with Art.

"Eight ball, corner pocket." Buddy leaned across the end of the table to line up his shot.

"Go for it."

Buddy eyed the line on the eight ball, drew back the cue, and drilled the shot. "Whew"—Art blew out his breath—"three in a row. Your game sure improved in jail… I mean."

Buddy stood up, resting the cue butt end by his foot. His face betrayed no reaction to Art's comment.

"I put some time in on it, that's for sure."

Art was visibly relieved. "Was it bad in there, Buddy, really?"

"Bad enough."

"Don't want to talk about it?"

"Nothin' really to say. Win some, lose some. Just stay alive."

"I'm sorry I asked."

"It's okay." Buddy looked around Chino's. "Everybody sure bailed out. Place is near empty."

"C'mon." Art put up his cue while Buddy did the same. "Let's sit at the bar a bit. I'll fill you in on the goin's on in Seco since you left. Maybe buy you a beer."

"Now you talkin', pal."

Back at Luke's

WHEN BUDDY GOT back to Luke's late in the afternoon, the old man was already home. Buddy tossed some supplies he'd bought for himself into the bunkhouse and went over to the main house for a visit. Luke's granddaughter Laci Jean met him at the door.

"Buddy!" the girl cried with delight.

Her exuberance caught Buddy off guard, and he had to gently disengage her arms from around his waist to get a good look at her.

"My God, Laci Jean. What a pretty young thing you've become."

"I ain't so young, anymore." She acted petulant.

"When I left you were just a little kid. But now…."

"Am I pretty?"

"Why, of course you are. You're the prettiest girl in Seco. By far."

"Buddy Harris,"—she wagged an index finger at him—"you are a big old liar."

"No, ma'am. I always tell the truth."

"Give Buddy some room there, Laci Jean," Luke grumbled as he came down the hall from the living room. "Stop actin' so boy crazy."

"Yes, Grandpa." Laci obeyed, but she gave Buddy a conspiratorial wink that the old man could not see.

"She sure has grown up, Luke," Buddy allowed, making the girl smile happily.

"Too darn much if, you ask me." Luke acted stern. "Get the boy somethin' to drink, girl."

"Yes, Grandpa."

"You got a Coke?"

"Get us all one."

"Yes, Grandpa."

"Let's sit a spell, Buddy. Catch up a bit."

"Yes, sir. That's why I'm back."

In the living room, Luke sat down in a big, heavy, old but comfortable-looking Barca-Lounger while Buddy plopped down on a cushion in a nearby rocking chair. When Laci Jean came back with the colas for everyone, she installed herself on a large sofa, at the end closest to Buddy.

He smiled at her. She looked back at him dreamily.

"I guess you know the details about your aunt's passin' and all?" Luke was slow to talk after a quiet spell during which the threesome slowly sipped on their cold Coca-Colas.

"Some, but it was hard to get real good information in there."

"Tell him about Patsy and Junior Emerson," Laci Jean butted in.

"Hush, child." Luke frowned.

"No need to tell about that one. Art Price squared me away on that at Chino's this afternoon."

"Well."

"I think it's just awful of her."

"Laci Jean." Luke leaned forward in his chair. "Please wait your turn. Let the grownups talk."

"Hmph." Laci Jean sniffed. Buddy restrained a laugh.

"I try to raise this girl right when she visits me, but she has way too many modern notions of her place in the world."

"I'm sixteen years old," Laci Jean proclaimed. "And I'm grown up enough for you two birds."

"Watch your tongue there."

"Yes, Grandpa. I'm sorry." Buddy took a drink of soda and check out the room.

"Anyway," Luke continued, "I was going to tell you what I know about your aunt, her passin', and her house sale and all."

"That would be good. I should know about that for sure."

"Well, you must know by now that Junior, blast his hide, bought it from your aunt Mary not long before she went into managed care."

"I hadn't heard about the managed care part, but I knew Junior bought it."

"She was taken good care of. Enough people in town knew and loved her to make sure of that."

"I appreciate it."

"Anyway, that Emerson boy, I imagine through some kind of wranglin' done by his uncle J. T., that no 'count scoundrel, bought your aunt's home. They didn't exactly steal it from her, but they didn't pay her top dollar neither. Still, there was a profit from the sale."

"Didn't know about that, either."

"Somewheres in the neighborhood of thirty-five hundred dollars as I recall. It was put in your name down at the First National in Seco."

"Wow, Buddy." Laci Jean whistled. "That's big money."

"Not so much nowadays, but it's a fair amount. My aunt was such a sweet lady. Treated me just as if I was her own boy."

"She was a wonderful woman." Luke agreed.

"She was real sweet to me, too," Laci Jean added.

"You'll probably want to check on that, first thing Monday," Luke suggested. "I wouldn't trust anything them Emersons had their hands into."

"I will, Luke, and I thank you for filling me in on it all. You're sure right about the Emersons, too. It must've set hard with 'em to have to leave anything to me at all. Especially after that poundin' I give Junior."

"They're the finaglin'est bunch in Seco, that's for sure."

"Why'd you beat up, Junior, Buddy?" Laci Jean was too young at the time to know anything more than that there had been a big fight, and it had cost Buddy his freedom.

"Hush, girl. That's none of your business."

"I'm sorry, Grandpa." Laci Jean teared up at the scolding.

"It's all right." Buddy held up a hand to tell Luke not to worry. "Me and Junior just had a disagreement over something we both wanted, that's all. I should have never done what I done. It's best to put it behind me."

"Solid thinkin', son."

"Still," Laci Jean declared, "I bet you he deserved it plenty. Those Emersons are just plain mean. Everybody knows that."

Working at Luke's

WHILE LUKE AND Laci Jean were at church in Seco on Sunday morning, Buddy used the quiet time to examine the outside of the house, barn, outbuildings, and the bunkhouse in order to get a fix on what kind of repairs might be needed. He figured he would earn his keep, besides helping with the stock and farm chores, by fixing up the outside problems first and then move inside to the interiors—bathrooms, lights, and so on.

It was the least he could do for the man who had done so much for him—taking him in when his folks had died in the car wreck and giving him the guidance that only a father could. Aunt Mary, as wonderful as she was, had no idea how to rein in a young boy like Buddy, and in the end even Luke had been unable to keep the boy from running afoul of the law. Although that law had clearly overstepped its boundaries and made an example of Buddy when somewhere else he might have gotten by with no more than a fine and a few days in the city jail for fighting. Buddy's mistake had been in whom he beat up, not why.

A little before noon Buddy finished up his check of the ranch buildings. He had found some cans of paint he could use for touchup, and there was wire for fence repairs, but he decided to make a run into Seco for nails and some other hardware for fixing doors and such. He figured he had enough money to at least do that for Luke.

On the way into town, his mind drifted briefly to his conversation with Art Price the day before. Even after all this time, which in some ways was like an eternity to him, he still had strong feelings about Patsy Mangrum—he just wasn't exactly sure whether those feelings were good or bad.

"I guess you heard the latest on Patsy and Junior Emerson, didn't you?" Art asked him as they sat at Chino's bar drinking beer.

"I ain't heard nothin' new."

"Oh, shit, sorry again."

"I figured things would be different. Changed. What happened?"

"They just got engaged."

"Uh-huh."

"Don't that piss you off?"

"It don't do anything to me."

"Well...."

Now, on the drive into town, Buddy knew he had not been fully honest with Art. It did bother him a little about Patsy and Junior. The irony of the situation was not lost on him. He had fought Junior for Patsy, beat him so badly that his uncle the sheriff had got Buddy put away for it, and now his ex-girl was engaged to the very punk who had caused all the trouble in the first place.

"Screw it." Buddy whipped his pickup into the gravel parking lot of the Panhandle Supply and Equipment store on the south end of town. "Why the hell should I care about any of this crap? I get my money Monday, I'm out of Seco for good. Albuquerque or bust."

He killed the motor, hopped out, and, with a cursory check of the parking lot, went inside the store.

Going to the Bank

MONDAY MORNING AFTER breakfast, Buddy took his leave of Luke again and headed straight downtown to the National Bank of Seco to find out about the money Aunt Mary had left him. He intended to get the cash converted to traveler's checks, spend a couple of days fixing up the barn and other buildings at Luke's, say goodbye to a couple of his friends, and head west to Albuquerque—out of the Texas Panhandle, away from Seco. There was an immediate hitch in his plans.

"I'm sorry, Mister Harris," the slight young banker informed him, "but there's a hold on that account."

"A hold?" Buddy noted the man's nameplate on his desk. "What the hell does *that* mean… Mister Taylor?"

"It means"—Taylor eyed the barbed wire tattoo on Buddy's right arm—"that the account has been frozen."

"Frozen. Frozen by who?"

"Uh, let me check with Mister Rodriguez." Taylor avoided eye contact. "He's our vice-president."

While Buddy and Mr. Taylor stood to one side of his desk, Mr. Rodriguez, a far more substantial man than his skinny subordinate, confirmed the hold on Buddy's account.

"It's right here in the file." Rodriguez spun his computer monitor around for Buddy to see.

"How can that be? Who can do that?"

"Let me check the details." Rodriguez clicked on an option on the screen. "Oh, yes, I thought I remembered."

"And?"

"Judge Aiken put a hold on this account at the request of the sheriff."

"They can do that?" Buddy scratched his head.

"Well, it's not standard or normal procedure, but in some cases, such as criminal activity, it can be done. I don't know your particular circumstances." He joined Mr. Taylor in eyeing the tattoo on Buddy's arm.

"What can I do about it?"

"I would suggest you take it up with the judge or with the sheriff. That would be the place to start. All we need is their say so and your account will be unfrozen."

"All right. I know where to start. Thank you, gentlemen."

"Our pleasure, sir."

Buddy rubbed his chin a moment, made a little bow to the bankers, then strode out of the building. The bankers watched Buddy until he had exited the building and, turning right toward the sheriff's office, disappeared into the bright Seco day.

A Chance Encounter

BECAUSE THE SHERIFF'S office was nearby, Buddy decided to leave his pickup parked by the bank and walk. About a block away from the office, he saw her. Patsy Mangrum, window shopping at one of Seco's last uptown stores, the relic of an old Five and Dime from many years ago. It was one of the last establishments that had not been shut down by the new mall and the big super shopping center that had been built at the edge of town.

She didn't see him at first. He just stopped walking and stood watching her from a few feet away. When she did see him, her face flushed bright red, and she became visibly agitated.

"Hello, Patsy."

"B—Buddy?"

"Same old."

"What… what are you doing here?" Patsy looked around. Buddy did as well. Nobody noticed them.

"Everybody's gotta be somewhere."

"You know very well what I mean." She scolded him,

"Didn't you hear I was back?"

"Yes, but…."

"But what?"

"But I didn't expect to see you."

"I can move on."

"That's not what I meant."

"Well, if it wasn't for your future uncle-in-law, you wouldn't have seen me at all."

"What does that mean?"

"Let's get a Coke over at the DQ there." Buddy pointed at a run-down Dairy Queen just up the street, yet another reminder of Seco's fading past and its new reality. "Sit down and talk a minute. Civilized like. I'll explain."

"I don't know."

"Come on, nobody cares if we talk for five minutes. I'll be gone soon enough."

At the DQ they managed to find a table outside under an awning that provided some relief from the sun. The kids working the place were too young to know about Patsy and Buddy, so they went on with their work without paying attention to the couple who resumed their talk.

"How's your family?" Buddy sipped soda from a medium-sized cup.

Patsy slowly scooped ice cream out of a small container with a plastic spoon. Buddy watched her familiar eating patterns, caressing the ice cream with her tongue before letting it dissolve in her mouth.

"They're all right."

"Momma and Dad? Little Amy?"

"Little Amy isn't so little anymore."

"How old is she?"

"Be fifteen in a couple of months."

"Good lord. Time does fly."

"I should be going." Patsy fidgeted.

"I haven't told you why I ran into you yet. You afraid to be seen with a criminal?"

"Stop that, Buddy."

"Okay."

"You were implying something about J. T., I believe."

"Yeah." Buddy explained. "Your intended and J. T. bought my

Aunt Mary's place just before she passed and while I was, uh, away. She left me some money."

"Well, that would be good, right? You can get that money and make a new start. Where'd you say?"

"I didn't say but was thinkin' of Albuquerque. Except J. T. put some kind of hold on that money, and without it I got nothin' to go on."

"Hold?"

"Yeah, hold. I was headin' up to see him when I ran into you."

"And that's all that's keeping you here?"

"You anxious for me to move on?"

"It's kind of uncomfortable, you know?"

"Not so uncomfortable to me. Me and you, sitting and talking. Seems pretty normal."

"That was a long time ago."

"I reckon so."

"I have to go, Buddy. I hope you get everything worked out. I really do."

"Uh-huh."

Patsy stood up. "Why did you come back, Buddy? You've been gone so long. Why come back now?"

"I didn't know where else to go," he answered honestly. "I was just going to say goodbye to Luke at first, see if I left anything here. Pay my respects to my aunt. I didn't know about the money till after I got here. But I can use it. I can use it to start over somewhere. I just picked Albuquerque 'cause it's far away from Seco. Now I want to get it, and blasted J. T.'s still messin' me up. Even after I done my time."

"You ain't bent on any kind of revenge, are you?"

"Naw, it don't mean nothin' to me. I just want the money. Nothin' else."

"You didn't come back for anything else?" Patsy sat back down.

"I might have…."

"Buddy, I waited the longest time for you. I did. But they said you wasn't ever goin' to get out. I thought I'd never see you again. I waited two years for you. It felt like forever."

"It was over two years. It has been forever."

"You can't blame me. I waited."

"I know you did, but Junior Emerson? How could you take up with him? After what happened?"

"I don't know. I don't know. I was lonely. He was good to me. You were never comin' home."

"I'm home now."

"I'm engaged to Junior." Patsy's eyes filled with tears. "I promised my word."

"Anybody but him."

"You were gone, never comin' back."

"I was fool enough to think you had waited. Stir time lets a man's mind wander too far, too far."

"I waited as long as I could." Patsy stood. "I've got to go. I hope you get your money, Buddy. I hope you have a good life."

"I wish…." Buddy began, but Patsy was already leaving him. She hurried away from the DQ. He stood up and watched her. She almost ran to the sidewalk on the other side of the street. "I wish I had never come back." Buddy completed his sentence, not with the idea on which it had begun.

He waited there by the DQ table for a few moments until Patsy had ducked into a store and out of sight. Taking a long, deep breath and at last standing up, he tossed his half-full soft drink into a trash receptacle and continued down the street toward the sheriff's office.

A Visit to the Sheriff's Office

"WELL, WELL, WELL." Deputy Carl Varela sized up Buddy when he walked into the Sheriff's Office out of the hot, glaring sun. "If it ain't Buddy Harris, the tough guy."

"Not so tough, Carl." Buddy walked up to the room's only desk, occupied by whichever official was on duty at the time. There were pictures of wanted men lying around on the desk, pencils carelessly tossed here and there, a big ashtray full of butts.

"No, I guess not." Carl grinned.

The two men had known each other most all their lives. Carl was the older brother of Tommy Varela, one of Buddy's teammates on the Seco High football team. Carl had not been around when Buddy had his famous run-in with J. T. and Junior Emerson.

"Sheriff around?"

"What ya need him for?"

"Private matter."

"You lookin' for trouble?"

"No. I just need to talk to Emerson. Private matter, havin' to do with money."

"Hmm." Carl raised an eyebrow.

"He around?"

"I'll see if he'll see ya. He's in back."

Carl jerked a thumb toward a closed door at the back left of the room, then rose and walked back to it. He poked his head inside and after a couple of seconds leaned back out.

"He says come on in, but make it snappy."

"It won't take long."

"Come on." Carl motioned with his left hand.

At the door he gave Buddy a quick frisk. When he was done, he smiled. "Clean," he called in to the sheriff, then motioned for Buddy to go in.

"Thanks." Buddy entered the doorway.

"Remains to be seen." Buddy stepped on into the sheriff's private room. Carl closed the door behind him.

Sheriff Emerson pretended to busy himself at a smallish desk occupying the back center of the little room. There was a half-empty bottle of soda on the desk beside a pile of papers. An oscillating fan blew warm air around. The walls had several pictures hung on them, mostly pictures of J. T. with local dignitaries, but one was with former Governor George W. Bush.

There were also the ubiquitous poster photos of Texas's most wanted outlaws. Buddy couldn't read what any of the criminals had done, but his jail time had given him a different perspective on the whole topic. He had a vague sense of empathy for the hunted lawbreakers. Finally, Sheriff Emerson looked up.

"You know, Harris. I had hoped never to see your face again, and now you're back in Seco. What the hell is it that you want?"

"Nice to see you, too, Sheriff."

"Can the bull. What are you here for?"

"Money. You know, the money my aunt left me from the, uh, *sale* of her house."

"That deal was on the up and up." Emerson was defensive.

"I'm sure it was. You all wouldn't take advantage of a little old lady whose only living relative you put in the pen, now would you?"

"Boy." Emerson rose red-faced, glaring menacingly. "You watch what you say. I'll put you right back in that pen if you ain't careful."

"Not if that sale wasn't as squeaky clean as a pair of new sneakers."

"It was clean, clean." Emerson throttled back some. "Nobody had nothin' against your aunt. We did the deal straight."

"Then why's the money she left for me held up? Why's that?"

"It was to be held up till you got out."

"I'm out."

"I ain't had time to get to the bank." Emerson sat back down.

"And I ain't leavin' till I get it. I'll get Rex Turner on it today if I have to."

"There's no need to lawyer up on it." Emerson leaned back in his chair. Buddy could see that the mention of Seco's only good defense lawyer was enough to give the sheriff pause. "Just take it easy."

"All right."

"You serious about leavin' Seco right away if you get that money?"

"Dead so. There's nothin' for me here anymore no ways. I don't even know why I came back. I didn't even know about my aunt's money."

"I'll get that money freed up, with conditions."

"What conditions?"

"You're a rotten apple, Harris. You were always trouble, and you always will be. You 'most killed my nephew."

"It was a fight, and I done my time for it. It don't appear you people ripped my aunt off too bad, but I want the money that rightfully belongs to me. I'm willing to fight you for it, though, with the law."

"Don't tell me about the law, you punk." Emerson flared up again. "I'll put your butt back in in a heartbeat."

"And maybe I'll take you with me this time."

"You threatenin' me?"

"I don't threaten. Ain't no value to it. 'Specially with a lawman."

"Better not, either." Emerson didn't seem to know if he'd won the point or not.

He took a swig from his soda and let the fan stir around the quieted down air. Buddy stared at the wall in back of the sheriff. There were the remains of a squashed cockroach or some other kind of big bug drying there. He could see a long, angular insect leg sticking out from the main squished mess. He looked away from the bug, back to Emerson. The sheriff returned the scrutiny.

"So you want the money?" Emerson leaned back in his chair again.

"That's it."

"Not revenge on me or Junior? Not to get your girl back? Not to avenge your aunt?"

"Do I need to avenge my aunt?"

"No."

"Well, that's good."

The sheriff leaned forward once more. Took another drink of soda. "This here's how you get your money, Harris, and the only way."

"I'm all ears."

"Number one, you keep away from Junior and Patsy. Don't mess with 'em at all." Buddy started to speak, but Emerson held up a hand to stop him. "And number two, the most important—you leave Seco and never come back. Go somewhere else."

Buddy kept quiet for a moment, acting as if he were mulling over the sheriff's conditions. Emerson watched him intently.

Buddy finally spoke. "Well, Sheriff, that should be just fine, 'cause I intend to do both of those things. Soon as I can on the leavin' part."

"The money will be yours tomorrow." Emerson audibly released a deep breath of air. "Then we're done here."

"We're done."

Buddy and Luke at the Black Gold

THAT EVENING BUDDY and Luke decided to drive into town to the Black Gold Café for supper instead of doing it themselves. They found an empty booth and had a cup of hot coffee while they waited on Rosa Avila to bring their order.

The place was pretty quiet, even for a Monday, and the two men held an easy conversation, Buddy shifting his gaze from time to time from Luke out to the nearly empty parking lot beyond the dusty windows of the café.

"I hate for you to have to leave for good." Luke set his cup on the booth table top. "Especially when you just got back and all."

"I reckon it's for the best."

"I suppose." Luke scrutinized the young man's face. Buddy looked up at him and then back out to the parking lot.

"I'd hoped to get more repairs done at the place."

"That don't matter, we were just hopin' you might be able to stay a while with us again, that's all."

"We?" Buddy peered at Luke over the edge of his own coffee cup.

"Me and Laci Jean."

"She's turned into quite a young woman." Buddy lowered his cup.

"I reckon she thinks you hung the moon or something."

"Well, she's pretty young."

"That's so, but she's a good judge of character, the trouble you been in be damned." Buddy laughed. "What's so funny?"

"Nothin', you just amaze me, that's all. You always stick by me, no matter what."

"Ahh."

"If I ain't mentioned it lately, Luke, I appreciate all you've done for me. Everything. Without you I don't think I would have made—"

"Nonsense." Luke cut Buddy off. "Every man deserves a place he can call home, no matter how good or bad he might be. And you're better'n most, regardless of the Emersons and the trouble they brung you."

"Well."

"You know," Luke held up a gnarled forefinger twisted by decades of hard farm and ranch work, "you can always come back. Emerson won't always be the sheriff. In fact, he's up for re-election next year. You wouldn't have to stay gone for good."

"That would be okay." Buddy looked up as Rosa arrived with their orders. "But you can't count on that happening."

"*What* happening?" Rosa flirted with Buddy while she set a plate of chicken fried steak, mashed potatoes and gravy, with a side of corn in front of Luke.

"You takin' off with me to New Mexico," Buddy teased Rosa.

She set his order, a quarter-pound cheeseburger and French fries, in front of him. He managed to run his hand along her arm as she did.

"Would you like anything else?" Rosa smiled. Buddy stared into her pretty dark brown eyes. After a moment, Luke coughed.

"Uh, ketchup, please, miss." Rosa giggled. Buddy looked at Luke, who stared back at him gravely. "Just ketchup, for now."

Rosa reached a bottle of ketchup from the booth behind Buddy and put it on the table in front of him.

"If you change your mind,"—she winked at both men—"you know how to find me."

"Ay, yay yay." Buddy watched her walk away.

"Maybe you have another reason to come back to Seco." Luke's eyes crinkled as he smiled.

"May be. May be."

The two men lapsed into silence then, concentrating on their meals. Luke ate slowly, deliberately, as he did most all things. Buddy went after his food with an energy bordering on vengeance. That was his normal way of doing things. He'd always been that way and didn't know why. He didn't think about it too often, though, it was just who he was.

Just as they were finishing eating, Buddy saw Cowboy Johnny Dupree pull into the parking lot in his battered old pickup. As usual, his younger cousin Lloyd was with him. The two young men spotted Buddy and Luke as soon as they entered the café.

"Hey, partner." Johnny hustled back to the table to exchange a high five with Buddy. Lloyd tagged along in his wake.

"Hello, sir." He knew to be polite to the old man.

"How are you, son?"

"Mister Miller." Johnny tapped the brim of his straw cowboy hat.

"Cowboy." Johnny's chest visibly swelled when the old man called him by his prized nickname. "You boys want to join us?"

"Thank you, sir, but no." Johnny politely declined. "Me and Lloyd here got some fence work to do out at Brennan's place, and we just gonna grab somethin' to go."

"Suit yourselves." Luke picked up his coffee. He took a sip and let the boys talk for a moment. Johnny sent Lloyd up to the counter to put in their order.

He had a proposition for his old friend.

"Listen, Buddy, I don't know what your plans are, but I got a line on some horse work. Over in Los Lunas."

"Los Lunas?"

"Yeah, you know, just south of Albuquerque. It's just below the town a few miles, off the interstate."

"Don't really know it."

"It's a nice place. Got a busy auction barn out west of town. I got a shot at company rider. I can get you work if you want it. They always need good men."

"I don't know."

"Well, just think about it. We can stay in touch through Luke, uh, Mister Miller. That would be all right wouldn't it, sir."

"Of course it would." Luke set his coffee down. "You bet."

"Okay then. I'll be expecting to hear from you."

"Well...." Buddy began.

"Gotta hustle, gentlemen," Johnny told them. "Looks like Lloyd's already got the order. See y'all."

"See ya."

"Remember goin' to the auctions over in Clovis?" Luke asked Buddy when Johnny and Lloyd had gotten their order and left.

"You betcha. They was always real polite folks. And friendly. But don't forget the times down in Lubbock or up in Amarillo."

"Amarillo." Luke stared off into the space beyond Buddy. "They got some fine women over there."

"All over Texas. 'Member that gal in Lampasas that time? Cowboy groupie we called her. Lord, sittin' on the railin' in them short skirts."

"She dipped Skoal, too." Luke laughed, remembering.

"And the back lot tradin', the craps games. That bunch of crazy boys from out by Lubbock that drove all the way to Santa Fe and back from Clovis drinkin', gamblin', and dealin' cattle."

"I do remember it all. Some I'd rather not."

"We had our times didn't we, Luke."

"I allow we did."

"I hate leavin' here without finishing fixin' up the place."

"You already done plenty, son. And you ain't gone just yet"

"No, sir, I ain't gone just yet."

Like a Bad Dream

BUDDY HAD TROUBLE sleeping after he and Luke got back to the ranch from supper. He tossed and turned, fretting and fuming about not getting enough done for Luke before having to leave, actually being *forced* out of Seco if a person thought about it.

Finally, sometime after midnight, he began to drift off. As he lay there in that place between sleep and consciousness, images and sounds began to fill up his mind, a scene from his not so distant past rising to the surface, unbidden.

"What are you doing here, Buddy?" He heard a girl's voice cry out to him.

"What are you doing with *him,* Patsy?" his own voice responded.

"You stay away from us." He heard Junior say. "Leave us alone."

"Shut up, Junior." He then turned on Patsy. "I work one weekend out at Luke's and you're with him already."

"Jenny Mathews was having her big graduation party. I had to go."

"Had to? What about now? You *had* to go to the DQ, with him, with Junior?"

"We're just getting burgers."

"She's with me now anyhow, Buddy."

"Shut up, Junior," Buddy growled.

"Watch your language in front of a lady," Junior spit back.

Buddy squared off at Junior, involuntarily moving his right arm from the shoulder down, clenching his right hand into a fist.

"I ain't afraid to fight you, Buddy."

Buddy feinted, Junior ducked, and Buddy backed off. "You ain't worth skinning' my knuckles on."

With a haughty look at Patsy, Buddy turned to leave, got maybe two steps before Junior grabbed a large Coke from somewhere, and launched it at his back. The full, soft plastic cup hit Buddy just below the neck and right between the shoulders, splattering ice and Coke all over his back.

"Son of a bitch." Buddy faced the now cowering Junior.

"Buddy," Patsy cried out. "Stop. Right now."

"Get out of my way." Buddy pushed her aside. Junior tried to retreat, but Buddy cut him off.

From that moment, until Sheriff J. T. Emerson, Junior's uncle, screeched up next to the fight in his patrol car and sprinted toward them with his night stick pulled and already swinging down at the back of his head, Buddy didn't know what he was doing. Patsy cried and tried to stop him, but in his blind fury he kept hitting Junior's battered, bruised, and bleeding face until he himself was hit so hard from behind that he could no longer swing anymore.

The next thing he knew he was coming to. He didn't realize until then that he had been knocked out, had lost consciousness. J. T. was standing over him, cursing, spitting, hitting down at him. Only a deputy pulling J. T. off saved Buddy.

The last thing Buddy remembered, before going out again, was the howling voice of J. T., the distorted visages of Patsy and the deputy, and a blurry image of red neon from the Dairy Queen sign behind them all.

By the time Buddy's wounds had fully healed, he'd already been convicted of felony assault and battery and was on his way to the joint. He got three years in prison, doing twenty-eight months before being let out on good behavior.

While in jail he vowed he would never do anything to wind up in stir again. Never. Ever. Now, jolted awake by the too-realistic dream memory of the fight with Junior, he lay in bed, sweat beading up on his forehead.

"Just a dream," he whispered to himself there in his bed, safe from jail and J. T. Emerson. He recalled his vow to himself from back then and letting out a long, deep breath, repeated it quietly like a mantra. "I'll never go back to that place. Never."

Another Visit to the Bank

AS SOON AS the bank opened Tuesday morning, Buddy was in line waiting to see Mr. Taylor, the young man he'd talked to before. And just as on the earlier visit, Mr. Taylor had to call over his supervisor, Mr. Rodriguez.

"Good morning, sir." The older banker smiled at Buddy, who was already starting to get a boil on but was trying really hard to control it.

"Uh-huh."

"Do we have a problem, Mister Taylor?"

"Well, sir." Taylor shrugged his shoulders. "Apparently Mister Harris's aunt's account is still not available to him."

"What? I thought that was already cleared up."

"I reckon I know the source of the problem. Just as you fellows no doubt do."

The two bankers considered Buddy with a mixture of surprise seasoned with a pinch of fear. Most everybody in Seco knew his story.

"Yes, sir?" Rodriguez raised an eyebrow.

"It's real simple." Buddy worked to maintain control of his emotions. He was fighting an urge to tear the place into little bitty bank pieces. "If you would be so kind, Mister Rodriguez, please get on the phone and call Sheriff J. T. Emerson for me."

"Yes, sir."

"And you tell that son of a bitch"—Buddy allowed himself a small safety valve of cursing—"that Buddy Harris is at the bank for his money, and if I don't get it right the hell now, I'm going straight over to Rex Turner's office and get myself lawyered up. And maybe I'll drop by the newspaper office just for good measure. Think you can tell him that for me?"

"Yes, I can, Mister Harris." Rodriguez exchanged a quick look with Taylor. "I'll just make the call from my desk. You don't mind?"

"Go right ahead."

Taylor tried a weak smile on Buddy. Rodriguez headed for his office. While Rodriguez was gone, Taylor busied himself on his computer, occasionally peeking over it. Buddy mostly fiddled around with his worn Texas Tech ball cap.

After five minutes or so, Rodriguez returned.

"Well?" Buddy asked as soon as the banker was back. "What did the lyin' sack of crap have to say?"

"The money's yours, Mister Harris." Rodriguez's tone was pleasant, but he was not smiling. "Mister Taylor here will take care of the account for you."

"Thank you."

"Good day to you, sir." Rodriguez turned and walked back to his office. Buddy turned his attention back to Taylor.

"And how would you like your money, Mister Harris?"

"Five hundred in cash. The rest in traveler's checks."

"And the cash, how would you like that?"

"Fifties." Buddy suddenly felt rich and happy. "Make 'em fifties. Yeah, that'll do."

"Yes, sir. Yes, sir, indeed."

Paying Respects

WITH HIS THIN, nearly worn out billfold overflowing with fifty dollar bills—making the right back pocket of his jeans fuller than he'd felt it in years—Buddy decided to drive just outside of town to pay some delayed respects. Just inside the gate of Seco's main town cemetery, he was stopped by its ancient caretaker, Mr. Baker.

"I'm going to visit the Harris plot. Irene and Jack."

"Just down the pavement there." The old man jabbed an age-twisted finger into the air. "Over by that old cottonwood tree. You can't miss it."

"Thank you, sir." Buddy didn't bother to remind the old man about who he was or that he had been to the cemetery many, many times before to visit the graves of his long dead parents. "I'm sure I won't."

Since the cottonwood was only about thirty to forty yards away, Buddy decided to park the pickup just off the pavement and then walk along the edge of the asphalt out to the gravesites. Out by the tall cottonwood, he turned back toward the caretaker. The old man gestured for him to go farther in. Buddy waved back and walked on, careful not to step on top of any of the graves.

In just a few moments he found his family. His parents' and his aunt's graves were next to one another, and he paused at the foot of the center one, that of his mother. His folks' graves were well settled, but Aunt Mary's, to his left, was—being only a year and some months old—still elevated above ground level. Buddy removed his cap and lowered his head.

After a brief, silent reflection before his mom and dad, gone so long now that the sharp pain of their loss had dulled to a permanent, small ache in his heart, he moved a step to his left and lifting his head, spoke out loud to the headstone of his late aunt.

"I'm sorry I wasn't here, Aunt Mary. I'm sorry you died alone. I didn't even know for weeks after. Not that they would've let me come, anyway." Turning his hat in his hand and looking around to see that he was alone, he went on with his little speech. "I thank you for your kindness to me when Mom and Dad died. I know I was more trouble than you could deal with. For that I'm sorry. And I know you hated to let me go to Luke's, but it was the best thing in the long run. Even with all the trouble that come down. But now you've given me another chance. Without this money, I don't know what I would've done. Now I'm free. Thanks to you. I thank you, and I love you, and if I ever find that those Emersons mistreated you in any way, I will come back and make them pay for it. I promise you that. I want you to know how grateful I am to you. You were a great aunt. I hope you know that. Thank you."

Letting out a deep breath, he stepped back from the graves. With a last, long look at the graves and headstones, he put his ball cap back on and walked out to the asphalt road and headed back to his car.

Delayed Gratification

BUDDY DROVE STRAIGHT from the cemetery to Carson's Western Store out on the main highway not far from the Black Gold Café. For the next half hour, a happy salesgirl fitted him out with a new pair of excellent quality cowboy boots, a couple of pairs of decently priced, straight-cut blue jeans, and three nice, long-sleeved cowboy shirts. Then she took him over to the western hat section, and they spent another fifteen minutes trying those on until he settled on a solid, well-made straw hat.

"This is a workin' hat."

The salesgirl was disappointed that he hadn't gone for a really good looking—and very expensive—Stetson. But when she rang up his total sale, her smile was back, and she joyfully took his money.

"Thank you very much, sir." She handed him back the change.

"Thank you. I haven't spent that much on myself in years."

As glad as he was to have some decent clothes again, he couldn't believe how much his shopping spree had eaten into his cash supply. Still, he hadn't had any good things to wear in nearly three years. He was probably entitled by now. Walking out of the store with his bags under one arm, he held his billfold out with his free hand and counted the remaining cash—just under three hundred dollars.

Outside, it was bright and sunny, and although he had just given himself a lecture about taking it easy with the money, he decided to give himself one more treat, a steak lunch at the Cattlemen's Restaurant across the road heading back into town. On the way, he had an idea. He pulled into a convenience store-gas station that had an outdoor bathroom, went inside and dressed himself in a set of his new clothes, with the new hat and boots, too.

"Yeah." He checked his new duds out in the smudgy bathroom mirror. "Lookin' good, lookin' sharp."

The Cattlemen's place was pretty busy, but he found a booth by himself, and when the waitress came for his order he chose a big Black Angus steak with baked potato and a small dinner salad. He settled for water to drink. It was the best meal he'd had since before prison, and he savored every single bite.

Being in his new clothes and all, and with pretty much everybody in Seco now knowing who he was, again, and with at least some theory about why he had come, he drew a few looks in the restaurant. But nobody said anything or bothered him in any way.

Nonetheless, he didn't stay long after he finished his meal, waiting just long enough to let the food settle in before deciding it was time to go spend some quality time with Luke out at the ranch.

Dropping a couple of bucks on the table as a tip, he smoothed down his new jeans, adjusted his new shirt, put on his perfectly fitting new hat, paid his bill, and walked out into the parking lot, careful not to scuff his new boots on any stair steps or stray rocks that might mar their fine, deep brown finish.

Putting Education into Practice

PREOCCUPIED WITH GETTING back to the ranch to show Luke his new duds, Buddy didn't see Junior and Patsy coming right at him out in the parking lot. Before he even knew they were there, Junior was up in his face.

"I thought Uncle J. T. done made it clear for you to get on out of town." Junior practically spit into Buddy's face.

"What the…?" He pulled back, startled.

"Don't, Junior." Patsy moved in front of him. "Don't."

Junior pushed her away and kept up his verbal assault. "You better be leavin' Seco, I mean right now."

"Ease up, hoss." Buddy began regaining his composure. He stepped toward Junior but made sure he didn't touch him.

"Buddy," Patsy cried. "Don't you do nothin'."

"I ain't doin' nothin'." Buddy was calm. "But you better put a muzzle on your pitbull here."

"You callin' me names, you bastard. I ain't afraid of you. You're nothin' but a dirty con. You don't belong in Seco anymore."

"You need to mellow out, sonny. You're gettin' yourself all worked up over nothin'."

"Nothin', huh?" Junior countered, sprays of spittle flying from his mouth. "I know why you come back. I *know.*"

"You do, huh?" Buddy laughed. "And what reason would that be? You tell me."

"You came back for her." Junior poked a finger in Patsy's direction.

"Oh, Junior." She groaned. "Right now, I wouldn't give a plug nickel for either one of you."

Buddy laughed again.

"That's funny to you?"

"Yes, Junior." Buddy's eyes narrowed. "It *is* funny."

"She's mine, not yours. She's *mine.* I got her while you were in jail. You're a loser."

"Step aside, boy, you're blockin' my pickup."

"You're yellow, that's what you are. You wouldn't a whipped me without sucker punchin' me. Try to sucker punch me now."

"We been here before." Buddy tried to step around him, but Junior shoved him as he went by. "Don't do that." Buddy lifted his left arm like a shield.

Junior squared up in front of Buddy in a fighting position. Buddy did the same. Junior flinched.

"You ain't worth it, son." Buddy lowered his hands. "You weren't back then, and you sure as hell ain't now."

With a dismissive wave of his hand, he walked past Junior to the pickup. Just as he did, the wail of Sheriff J. T. Emerson's patrol car split the Seco air.

"Damn."

J. T. hopped out of the police car and headed straight for Buddy, nightstick in hand.

"Stop right there, Harris."

"Oh, hell." Buddy dropped his arms by his sides and slowly turned to face the advancing sheriff.

"I warned you to keep away from them." Emerson thumped his nightstick menacingly against his own palm.

"I…."

"No excuses, Harris. You got your money, I know that. You should be gone by now."

"I'm supposed to be gone already? How in hell…?"

"Don't you swear at me boy." Emerson pushed his nightstick into Buddy's chest. "Don't you swear at me. I'll bust you right now."

"Leave him alone, Uncle J. T.," Junior interjected. "I can take care of myself. I was handlin' him before you got here."

Buddy rolled his eyes.

"It ain't a matter of that, Junior. This punk is on probation, and he's in violation of his terms."

"Not true," Buddy countered.

"Shut up, boy."

"I was gettin' ready to kick his ugly ass, Uncle J. T., right when you showed up."

"Is that right?" Buddy sneered at Junior. Both men advanced on Buddy, who brought his arms up into a fighting position with both fists clenched tight.

"Stop it." Patsy threw herself between the Emersons and Buddy. "Stop it right now. Buddy never touched Junior."

"Why are you defendin' him?" Junior whined. "You still love him, don't you?"

"Oh, Junior, just shut up. I do *not* still love him."

"It don't matter." Sheriff Emerson moved back a step. "I made it abundantly clear that he's to stay away from you all, from both of you."

"He was just coming out of the restaurant, Sheriff." Patsy explained. "He didn't come looking for us, we ran into him."

"Crap," Junior groused.

Sheriff Emerson turned to his nephew. "Is that true, Junior?"

"Well… I reckon."

The sheriff lowered his nightstick. "Hell."

"Sheriff, after I got my money this morning I bought me some new clothes and then came here to have a big meal. I run into these guys on my way out. That's all, I swear."

There was a long pause while the sheriff considered the situation. After a while he put the nightstick back on his duty belt, adjusted his pants, and cleared his throat.

"We had an agreement, Harris. You were given a warning. I expect you to get out of town, uh, soon."

Buddy looked at Patsy and Junior. They stared at their feet. He turned to the sheriff.

"Yes, sir. That is exactly what I plan to do."

On Luke's Back Porch

WHILE LUKE AND Laci Jean had a big supper of meat, potatoes, and beans topped off with peach pie and a big glass of cold milk, Buddy settled for lighter fare, a tuna fish sandwich on plain wheat bread and a coke. Between his big lunch at the Cattlemen's Restaurant and the excitement of the subsequent parking lot run-in with the Emersons, his appetite had been considerably diminished.

He knew as long as J. T. Emerson was the local sheriff, Seco could no longer be his home. He accepted that reality, but it made him a little melancholy, a little moody, especially considering Luke's advanced years. If he were gone too long, he might never see the old man again. It was not a good thing to think about.

"Are you sad, Buddy?" Laci Jean sat on the top step of Luke's back porch where the three of them had retired after supper.

Luke sat in a rocking chair, his long legs stretched out before him, his eyes closed. Buddy was a few feet to his right in a straight-backed chair with a woven-cane seat. They had intentionally left the porch light off to discourage bugs, and the only lights beginning to shine in the dim light were those out beyond the horse and cattle stalls and the other ranch outbuildings and those from nearby spreads. Overall, it was turning into a pleasant evening, cool enough to be comfortable, with a light wind providing an occasional breath of fresh air.

"What?" Buddy slowly realized he had been spoken to.

"I asked if you was sad." Laci Jean repeated.

"No, no." Buddy lied a little. "Just thinkin' of things."

"Are you thinkin' you should've beat up that stupid Junior Emerson again?"

"No."

"Him and that stupid sheriff uncle of his, well, they're just old bastards, anyway."

"Watch your language, young lady." Luke emphatically corrected his granddaughter.

"I thought you were asleep, Grandpa. I'm sorry. But it's true. They're rotten men."

"Young girls nowadays," Luke pronounced. Laci Jean suppressed a twitter. Her grandpa was always saying things like that about modern times and modern people, but she knew she was his favorite. He just liked to act like a grumpy old man sometimes. "What do you make of them, Buddy?"

"I think some of these young girls are sort of all right, Luke." Buddy winked at Laci Jean, which she happily saw in the fading light.

"Well, I suppose. But you were right not to fight that Emerson boy again. Nothing good would've come from it, and it would've played right into their hands. You'd a sunk back to their level."

"Buddy couldn't never be at their level, Grandpa, no matter what he done."

"He's smart, girl. He learned. Now he can start his life off again. But we'll miss you somethin' terrible, I have to admit."

"We sure will." Laci Jean agreed.

"I wish I'd had more time to fix the place up for you, Luke." Buddy tried to skirt the sentimentality that threatened to overcome him.

"That's all right, son. It's okay. I appreciate what you got done."

There was a lull in the conversation then as each of them there on the porch considered what Buddy's leaving would mean.

Laci Jean broke the silence. "We'll be here if… no, *when* you come back to us, Buddy."

"Maybe we will." Luke emphasized the "maybe." He was realist enough to know that, given his age, his time might be up any day.

"Oh, Grandpa." Laci Jean lovingly chided Luke. "You're gonna live forever. Right, Buddy?"

"He better."

"You two kids." Luke laughed.

"We love you, Grandpa." Laci Jean rose and walked over to the old man. She leaned down and hugged him.

"All right. That's enough of this nonsense. I've got to get some rest. Let's not say goodbye at all. We'll just pretend Buddy's going away for the weekend or something. That he'll be back real soon."

"That's the spirit, Grandpa." Laci Jean patted the old man's hand.

"Y'all help me up, now, will you? Things'll be better tomorrow, after a good night's sleep." Laci Jean and Buddy hustled to help Luke to his feet. "Only one thing I ask, Buddy."

"Shoot." Buddy lifted Luke up. Laci Jean helped steady her grandpa.

"Come back to us as soon as you can, and if I'm gone, take care of this girl, will you? She's a wild one."

"Grandpa." Laci Jean laughed.

"I promise." Buddy vowed. "On both accounts."

"Well."

"Well, indeed, Grandpa." Laci Jean studied Buddy's face as they walked Luke into the house. "Very well, indeed."

Leaving

BUDDY WOKE UP early, ready to go. The first thing he thought of was that he hadn't checked with anybody about his parole status. To hell with that he decided, I can do it in New Mexico—or not at all. If they want to come after me, fine. I won't be hiding.

As he went about getting his few things together, he tried to be as quiet as he could. He didn't want to wake up Luke or Laci Jean—he'd already said goodbye to them the night before and didn't want to do it again. He took his stuff out to the kitchen and made himself toast and coffee as silently as possible, lifting a couple of slices of cold ham out of the refrigerator for protein and downing a small glass of milk to cut the aftertaste of the coffee.

Walking down the hall to the front door, he couldn't help but check in on Luke. He knew the old man was awake, he was always an early riser, but when Buddy ducked his head into the bedroom door, the old man was doing a good job of pretending to still be asleep. Smiling, Buddy quietly got his belongings and headed down the hallway to the front door.

He listened as he passed Laci Jean's bedroom, but there was no sound—he figured a young girl like her would sleep late—and so he closed the front door gently and walked across the yard to his pickup. The ignition turned right over, and he shoved the floor shift into low gear. He was just pulling out of the driveway when the front door of Luke's banged open, and Laci Jean, in her nightgown, came racing out of the house.

"Buddy," she cried. "Buddy. Wait." He braked and pushed in on the clutch. Laci Jean darted in front of the pickup and over to his window, which he rolled down. "Don't you dare leave without telling me goodbye."

"I thought you were still asleep."

"Don't be silly."

"I wasn't tryin' to sneak out on you."

"You come back to us, now, soon. Okay?" She bent to the window of the pickup and gave Buddy a sweet kiss, right on the mouth.

"Wow." Buddy whistled.

"You come back and I'll be grown. Don't forget me."

"Not likely." Buddy reached out and briefly held her hand. "Not too darn likely."

"Bye, Buddy."

"Bye, kiddo. I'll see you again."

"You better."

"I will." Buddy promised.

Laci Jean stepped back from the pickup. Buddy began to drive forward again.

"Be sure to tell Luke I said goodbye," he called as he pulled away.

"I will… I will."

Buddy reached the main road and turned right. As he hit the gas for the drive back into town, he glanced back at the house one more time. Laci Jean was in the front yard waving and for just a flash of a moment he thought he saw the gaunt, tall figure of Luke framed in the front window, but after looking up at the road and then back to the house, there didn't seem to be anyone there after all. With a final wave in the general direction of the house, he put his foot to the gas and headed for Seco.

A Last Visit to the Toast

AFTER FILLING UP the truck at a convenience store service station on the highway in Seco, Buddy drove out to the Black Toast to get a sandwich and a soda for the road. He recognized a few workingmen in the crowded café, including Clu Tucker with whom he exchanged friendly greetings. Del Holland was at his usual place behind the cash register, and Rosa Avila was working behind the counter. Sitting down at the counter, Buddy signaled to Rosa.

"Hi, Buddy." She leaned against the counter and smiled sweetly. Buddy couldn't help but give her lovely chest a pleasant once over. She winked at him. "What'll it be, good lookin'?"

"You want to run away with me, Rosa? Maybe go to New Mexico?"

"Right now?"

"Why not?"

"Well, sugar." Rosa gathered herself from the surprise invitation. "I can't just go traipsing off with the first handsome cowboy who asks me, now can I?"

"Why not?" Buddy repeated.

"Buddy, you're a sweet man, but you know I have to stay in Seco and take care of my momma and my little nephews and all."

"Sure." Buddy smiled. "Can't blame me for tryin', though, can you?"

"You're sweet. I'm flattered you asked."

"Flattered enough to give me a raincheck?"

"You got it."

"Don't be surprised if I don't use that raincheck one of these days."

Rosa winked at him again. "Now what can I get for you today? Chicken fried steak? Fish Fry?"

"No, just get me a steak sandwich and a big Coke to go.

"Are you really going to New Mexico? Right now?"

"I am."

"I'll get your order right out, honey."

In the Parking Lot

ON HIS WAY out of the café, Buddy waved to Rosa one last time, paid Del at the register, and then stepped back to deliver a message for Clu Tucker to pass on to Johnny Dupree.

"You see Cowboy, tell him I took him up on his New Mexico lead."

"You bet, Buddy." Clu shook his hand. "Good luck to you, pardner."

"See ya." Buddy tipped his hat to the other men at the table as he headed out of the café.

He was just about to crank the engine when another pickup suddenly pulled up to his left, its driver side next to and parallel to his. It was Patsy Mangrum. Buddy let out a little sigh and rolled his window down. Patsy had done the same on her truck.

"I was just out at Luke's." She began by way of explanation. "Laci Jean guessed you might be stopping here last."

"Well," Buddy drawled, "I reckon she guessed right."

"Don't be mad at me."

"Hell, I ain't mad at nothin' at all. Just leavin', simple as that."

"I'm sorry about Junior and J.T."

"Old news. 'Sides, it ain't got that much to do with you, not really."

"Do you forgive me, though?"

"Nothin' to forgive."

"But do you?"

"Sure, I guess."

"Doesn't sound very convincing."

"I suppose I hadn't thought about it that way, Patsy. It's closed out for me now. I'm leavin'. No regrets. It's all behind me."

"Really?" Patsy didn't sound convinced.

"I reckon."

"Well...."

"Well...."

There was a pause before Patsy spoke again.

"I wish you good luck."

"You, too." There was another pause.

"Buddy...." Patsy started, then stopped. He could see tears welling up in her eyes.

"Yeah?"

"Be safe. Be happy."

"Same for you."

"Goodbye." She shifted her pickup into gear.

"So long, Patsy."

Without another word, Patsy revved up her pickup and hurried out of the parking lot onto the highway and headed back into town. Buddy didn't move for several minutes. He just sat there in his truck, staring blankly out the windshield. The café's red and white neon sign blinked off and on from time to time, but Buddy didn't notice. Finally, he started the engine, pulled out of the lot and onto the highway, heading in the opposite direction from Patsy.

Seco in His Rearview Mirror

SPEEDING DOWN THE highway away from Seco, Buddy smiled to himself. He had gone home and faced all the old demons. And he had come out okay. He had not repeated the same old mistakes. He had wanted to, but he didn't. Like Luke had said the night before, he had actually learned and put that learning into practice. Maybe it was that, or maybe he was a little bit more mature, or maybe it was just not wanting to go back to jail. Whatever it was, it didn't matter now. He had done it, and now he was leaving.

He regretted leaving Luke, whom he might never see again, and Laci Jean, who he was sure he would, and Rosa, and… well he would most likely run into Cowboy Johnny Dupree on the horse circuit somewhere, sometime. He still had some friends, he had his old pick-up, a few dollars in his pocket, and a future. Yes, he still had a future. Somewhere other than in Seco, but a future nonetheless.

Buoyed by his newfound hope for a new start and an unexpected feeling of overall wellbeing, Buddy considered his hometown in the rear-view mirror. It seemed small and claustrophobic. Confining. Limiting.

He knew it was time to get while the getting was good. Time to make a new life for himself. With a low cry of celebration, he put his foot down hard on the gas pedal.

He was out of there.

COWBOY

THE PILE OF beer cans outside Johnny Dupree's little trailer made it appear like he was the collection point for a one-man recycling program. The small refrigerator inside always had at least a twelve-pack in it, and when he emptied a can, he just opened the trailer door and tossed it onto the growing pile.

The trailer had an old hot plate in it for heating up pork and beans and such, but he preferred eating at the Los Lunas Horse and Cattle Auction Barn snack bar across the dirt road and sandy parking lot from his trailer.

His full name was John Martin Dupree, but those who knew him best called him Cowboy because he was one of the finest horsemen in the southwest. He always had a girl or woman hanging around—of late a young half-Navajo, half-Mexican girl named Luisa.

Johnny had come to Los Lunas from Seco, Texas, via a pretty circuitous route. Along with his little sister Kate, he was a late arrival in the life of his elderly father, Preston. Preston Dupree himself was a well-known horseman in the Seco area, and he raised his boy and girl on the family spread just outside the dusty Texas town. Mrs. Dupree died when Kate was only two and Johnny five, and the old man raised both kids to be horse ranchers like himself.

When Kate was nine she took a bad fall from a high-strung buckskin, and her health was never the same after that. She still worked with the old man on the ranch, but she had complications from the accident and pain spells that left her a near invalid.

For his part, Johnny took to the cowboy life like the proverbial duck to water. From the time he was ten or eleven there was hardly a horse he ever saw that he couldn't ride, tame, or intimidate into well-trained submission.

Like his fellow cowboys, he lived day to day, never caring to have much more than a good meal or two each day, enough coin to buy some beer, and a woman when one was needed. This life went on happily, and unabated, until the year his father passed away.

The old man had been declining as early as Johnny's high school years, and though he was as old as the grandfathers of most of the other boys his son's age, Preston Dupree's death hit the boy real hard. Knowing his father wasn't there to watch him took some of the pleasure out of riding a three-fourths tame quarter horse full speed into the tiny fenced in plots of dirt that stood as show arenas at most of the auction houses. And he wouldn't see his boy put the animal through its paces like it was the calmest, best mannered mount in the desert southwest.

Eventually, Johnny moved on to New Mexico and within a few months sent for his sister. He set her up in a decent, easily accessible apartment on the southeast side of Albuquerque, and though he usually only saw her once a week or so, just having her nearby gave him a family base, a solid place he could depend on now that the old man was gone. Without his dad, he felt half of him had been cut out. Without Kate, he didn't know what, if anything, might be left of him.

"What'll it be, Cowboy?" Sherry, the lady who ran the snack bar in the auction barn, asked when Johnny clomped up to the counter in his dusty boots. He was limping slightly from a bone spur on the side of his left ankle, but it was not the cowboy way to show pain, much less talk about it.

"Gimme some of them flapjacks you got there, Sherry, please."

It was Thursday morning, and the early arrivals for the weekend sale would be coming in by mid-morning. Johnny knew he might go a long time before he'd have another sit down meal so he ordered big.

"And a couple of eggs, hash browns, a slice of ham, and toast."

"Coffee?"

"Yes, ma'am."

"How you like your eggs?"

"Broken."

"Very funny."

"Scrambled, if you please."

"White or wheat on the toast?"

"Wheat."

"Go ahead and sit down." Sherry pointed to a corner of the snack bar where several of his cohorts were holed up. "We'll bring it out to you."

"I really do appreciate it, ma'am." Johnny tipped his hat. "Thank you very much."

"Go on now." Sherry laughed. "'Fore all that cowboy politeness gets you into trouble."

"Mornin', boys." Johnny greeted his cowboy friends at the corner table. "Wonderful day today."

"Can it, Dupree," a really big Mexican kid everyone called Pancho told him. "We heard all that crap you feed these women already." The other men at the table snickered.

Besides Pancho, there was Wayne, an older wrangler, who mostly worked back in the pens, cutting out animals for the main riders and helping the vet do the required bloodletting for each horse up for sale. It was required that every horse have a clean Coggins test, which determined if the animal had what might be termed Horse Aids.

If an animal tested positive, well that was the end of that. Every horse in the general vicinity would be quarantined. It was a terrible test to fail. Luckily failures were very, very rare. Neither Johnny nor any of the other hands had seen a horse fail the Coggins, but they'd all heard the horror stories of ones that did.

Also at the table was Givers, the young yard boss who was super-organized and excellent with figures—a necessity anywhere large numbers of animals would be bought and sold. Sitting by Givers was a short, heavy Navajo wrangler whose real name was Martin Begaye. All the cowboys and wranglers had renamed him Cool Daddy because of his amazing ability to calm and handle the wildest of auction horses, even the nearly feral ones called Brumbies.

"Nice seein' you fellas, too." Johnny pulled a chair up beside Givers who was jotting down numbers and names in a small notebook. "What you doin', Givers, 'work stuff?'"

"Yeah. CB wants a list of everybody working back in the pens and what they're supposed to be doing. You know CB."

"I—CB—M, you mean." Wayne laughed. "The guided missile."

"Crazy Bastard, you ask me," Cool Daddy chipped in.

"Nobody did." Johnny took a playful swipe at Cool Daddy, who feigned fear. "You no 'count Injun."

"I kick your ass, white cowboy Johnny." Cool Daddy laughed. Johnny chuckled.

Charles Beltre was the man the cowboys called CB or ICBM, the guided missile. Beltre was the owner of the Los Lunas Livestock Auction, including the land, the pens, and the auction barn itself. He was a hard driving, self-made man, and he intended to make a go of the auction, come hell or high water.

CB was renowned for his quick temper and quick decisions, which usually led to the rapid firing and even more rapid rehiring of his workers. Every one of the men at the snack bar table had felt Beltre's wrath and forgiveness—usually more than once.

After breakfast, all of them save Pancho—who was moving hay using a four-wheel drive ATV with a forklift attachment that morning—hopped into Givers's pickup and headed for the back pens where the veterinary testing was just beginning for the day.

The wranglers climbed the fence and dropped down into the wide pen. The vet and a vet lab tech were drawing blood from an assortment of quarter horses that Wayne and Cool Daddy quickly began to move, one at a time. They guided them through a series of chutes and gates leading up to a last one where the blood was removed, sometimes at the risk of physical injury to the animal, or even the vet or lab tech.

If a horse was particularly rambunctious or dangerous, Cool Daddy would slip a rope around its neck and head and with his powerful arms and legs and soothing manner bring the horse under control. He was doing that very thing when Johnny walked up to the chutes.

"Nice work, Cool Daddy." Johnny had hung back a bit to watch the bleeding and to maybe ask the vet about the painful spur on his foot.

"You come hold 'im, Cowboy." Cool Daddy laughed, sweat pouring off his face. Smiling, Johnny declined the offer.

"Hey, Cowboy." Wayne lifted his head for Johnny to check behind them at a woman climbing up onto the fence around the pen. All the men turned to watch.

"There you go." Jeffrey "Doc" Crasner, the vet, laughed. "There's Judy, the cowboy groupie."

Johnny watched the woman as she made it to the top of the fence and sat with her legs out, just barely concealing herself in a very short, and out of place, skirt. She smiled at him and the other men. He turned away and spat. Her smile faded.

"Man." Wayne leaned against the chute. "What a body."

"She may have a helluva body," Johnny deadpanned, "but she got the face to guard it with, too."

The other cowboys laughed. That was vintage Cowboy. No woman ever put anything over on him.

BY MID-AFTERNOON THURSDAY, the auction was getting pretty busy. Doc Crasner and the vet lab tech were kept busy by the unexpected arrival of a load of nearly sixty Brumbies off a western New Mexico government reserve. They needed Wayne and Cool Daddy's help most of the time with the nearly-wild animals. Givers was in the back pen, too, keeping track of the Brumbies and the increasing stream of quarter horses destined for the main horse sale.

Up in the auction barn, buyers were beginning to gather, and the fast-talking, high energy auctioneers and their ring men around the arena tried to work up enthusiasm for the first few horses brought out for sale. Pancho joined Johnny in showing most of the animals, and they kept up a joking banter between themselves and with the back-up auctioneers, ring men, customers, and the many others hanging around the show pen inside the auction barn itself.

Charles Beltre, CB, stomped around the grounds barking unnecessary and mostly unheeded orders to his cowboys, wranglers, and anyone else who even appeared to be working for Los Lunas Horse and Cattle Auction.

Late in the afternoon, during a lull, Johnny was riding a smallish Bay in the dirt runways between the pens toward the back of the auction yard when he saw Doc Crasner walking toward him. He pulled the Bay alongside the metal pen to his right and waited for Crasner.

"Hey, Doc."

"Hey, Cowboy."

"Got a minute?"

"Sure, Johnny, always got time for you."

"Well, Doc." Johnny reached down by his left boot. "I got me a lump or something there on my foot that is just killin' me. Sometimes when I really kick it to a horse, the pain near blinds me. Think you can help me?"

"Well, Cowboy, you gotta remember I'm a veterinarian, not an M.D. I can't practice on humans."

"I know that, Doc, but I thought you might be able to help me some, you know, unofficial like and all."

"Well, I tell you what. You come see me Sunday afternoon when the place is clearin' out and I'll check that foot for you. I'll even recommend a real human doctor for you down in Socorro."

"Thanks, Doc. That'd be a real help."

Later in the day, Johnny was showing a beautiful four-year-old Palomino mare in the show arena when he first saw the woman. She was at the south end of the arena, dressed like a Spanish riding lady—all in black with gold buttons on the sides of her tight pants and on the front of her even tighter blouse—and wearing a round wide-brimmed black hat. Her dark brown hair was cut stylishly short above her shoulders, and her full lips were parted in an enigmatic smile.

Her dark eyes sparkled at Johnny's open-jawed admiration of her lovely brown skin, her high cheekbones, and thin, perfectly proportioned nose. All in all, she cut what Johnny thought his sister Kate might describe as an "exotic" figure—a fancy woman. Only CB's high, rasping voice managed to break his lock on this new vision of loveliness.

"Damn it, Cowboy." CB cursed from just outside the auction barn back entrance. "Get that animal in there or I'll fire you right now. And, by God, don't think I won't."

Without a word, Johnny spurred the Palomino to breakneck speed and shot into the small show arena. At the side of the pen nearest the fancy woman, Johnny pulled hard left on the reins, and the horse responded, turning on a dime and then galloping back to the pen entrance. He turned the animal once more, rode her slower across the arena, pulled her to the right this time, and then jogged her back toward the entryway. Finally, he pulled both reins toward himself, walking the Palomino backward through the deep dirt of the pen. The mare was a fine horse, and it was a good show ride.

The auctioneer's energy picked up, and the ring men went to work on driving up the price for the horse. With a long gaze at the fancy woman in black, Johnny trotted the horse out of the arena.

"Did you see that woman in there?" he asked Pancho after dismounting and releasing the Palomino into a holding pen. Pancho had.

"I think she's from Albuquerque. Rich. And trouble."

"The kind of trouble I could stand."

Suddenly, CB emerged from the auction building, coming at them like one of the missiles for which he had been nicknamed.

"Look out," Pancho warned, but it was too late.

"Get the hell back out to the vet pen," CB shouted at Johnny by way of greeting. "And get that big Bay in the far southeast pen with the Rockin' H brand. Get 'im and get 'im up here right now."

"A big Bay?" Johnny was a little confused by the order.

"I know the one," Pancho said.

"Cowboy, do it right now," CB demanded.

"Geez." Johnny turned to go. "Give me a break."

"Bring him back up here… ASAP."

"Geez." Johnny took off at a fair pace, limping from the bone spur.

As soon as CB was back in the auction barn, Pancho hustled over to his fork-lift mounted ATV, started it up, and whipped the small vehicle into the runway down which Johnny had gone.

"Hop on, Cowboy." He pulled the ATV up close behind Johnny. "I'll give you a ride back to the pens."

"Thanks, Pancho." Johnny was relieved not to have to walk on his sore ankle any farther. "I appreciate it, brother."

JOHNNY FOUND THE Bay and, after loosening the horse up for a couple of minutes in the runway near the back pens, walked it up to the auction arena. CB was waiting for them, eyes blazing. Pancho stood to one side watching the whole show.

"Get off." CB flailed his arms at Johnny. "Get down. Get out."

Johnny almost laughed at his boss's apoplectic outburst. "What the hell are you talkin' about, CB?"

"I told you to get that Bay right back up here." CB nearly frothed. "Now get off of him. You're done."

"I'm done?" Johnny slid smoothly out of the saddle. He stepped down onto the dirt in front of CB. Johnny's thick frame made CB appear even smaller than he actually was.

"Fired," CB hissed. "Fired. You're *fired.* I warned you."

"For God's sake, I got up here as fast as I could. I had to warm him up some."

"Don't care. Go on. You're through."

"All right. You're the boss."

"That's damn straight. I'm the boss."

"There's just no pleasin' you today, CB. No matter what I do. I'll be in my trailer when you need me."

"Won't need you." CB spoke to the back of Johnny's head, as the young rider limped on into the auction barn. *"Don't* need... you're fired."

Without turning back, Johnny waved his left arm as if to indicate his own dismissal of the scene. Pancho stood where he had been, a few feet from CB, trying to stay out of trouble.

When CB noticed him, he jumped him next. "You got a problem, big man?"

"No, sir." Pancho smiled broadly. "I'm just fine."

"Then get on that Bay and show it. Now."

"You bet, CB." Pancho mounted the horse. "You bet."

As Pancho headed the Bay toward the show arena, Johnny Dupree was going out the front, west side of the barn. He walked slowly toward his trailer, favoring his left foot. At the door of the trailer, he paused. Luisa was hustling toward him across the sandy, dirt lot, and behind her, framed for just a moment in the door of the auction barn, he could see the fancy lady looking out at him. Something made Luisa look back just then herself, and the other woman ducked back into the barn. Johnny went on to the trailer without waiting for Luisa.

JOHNNY WAS STILL asleep, Luisa buried in the covers beside him, when CB started banging on the trailer door the next morning.

"What?" Johnny mumbled, sliding part way out of bed. The banging on the door became louder, more insistent. "All right, all right."

"Cowboy." He heard CB outside. "Get up. I need you at the barn. C'mon, I know you're in there."

Johnny stood up by his bed, groaned a little from the soreness caused by the bone spur, but managed to get into his work jeans without too much trouble. He stumbled to the door, yawning and stretching. CB kept on banging away at the trailer.

"What the hell?" Johnny pulled the door open. He squinted into the early morning light.

"Get your shirt and boots on, Cowboy, we've got a big day comin' and I need you to show a Palomino right away."

"Hold on, CB. You fired me yesterday, remember? I don't work here no more."

"Yes, you do, damn it. You're hired back. Right now."

"I want yesterday's pay, too."

"Yes, yes, all right. Just get over there. There's money to be made."

Before there was time to work up any further response, CB darted away, heading for the auction barn, double time. With a laugh, Johnny closed the trailer door.

FRIDAY WAS A very busy day at the Los Lunas Livestock Auction. Better than one hundred and eighty quarter horses were shown and bid on in the auction barn, and well over four hundred new animals arrived during the day and were given the mandatory Coggins test.

Buddy Harris, Johnny Dupree's old friend from Seco, Texas, came in early and spent the day splitting time between showing horses in the arena and helping wrangle the steady stream of animals getting their blood checked. Doc Crasner and his partner, the vet lab tech, worked nearly non-stop all day taking blood from the animals.

As the work waned in the lengthening shadows of late afternoon, Johnny made a trip around the pens to line up the crew for a cowboy's Friday night out. Cool Daddy was all for it, as were Wayne and Buddy. Pancho begged off, but Givers said he'd make it, though a little late as he had to catch up on some paperwork before he could go out.

Johnny chose the Blue Moon, a country and western bar in nearby Belen, for the gathering. By a quarter to nine the whole crew was at the club swilling Budweisers like the hard working, thirsty men they were.

Standing by the long L-shaped bar with the boys, across the room he saw Doc Crasner, the vet lab tech, and a guy who'd been helping the lab tech with the furious testing of the newly arrived horses during the day. They waved at Johnny, and he raised his beer in greeting. He was about to saunter over for a quick visit when a woman suddenly materialized in front of him.

"I hear they call you Cowboy."

He was only a little surprised that she was the fancy woman he had been seeing at the auction for the last two days.

"Some do." He took a swig of beer. Buddy Harris was down the bar from him and gave a shake of his head when Johnny saw him. Johnny ignored the signal.

"Is that because you're good in the saddle?"

"Could be." He lowered his beer.

"I like a man who's not afraid of a good ride."

"I reckon I can do a good ride."

"I bet you can."

"Johnny's my name. Johnny Dupree. Most of the boys *do* call me Cowboy, though."

"How appropriate. I'm Marcie Philips." She extended a well-manicured hand.

"Nice to meet you." He took her small, soft hand in his thick, rough one.

"Shall we dance?"

"I'm game."

"I was hoping you would be." She pulled him out toward the dance floor. "I like my men game."

"Yes, ma'am." Johnny gave Doc and the boys a "what can I do?" wave, which they returned. "No doubt you do."

Over at Doc's table there was an appreciative nodding of heads at Cowboy's apparently effortless and quick conquest.

"Look at that son of a gun." Doc laughed. "He's smoother'n a brand new colt's rump."

"Remarkable," the vet lab tech added.

"Darned near amazing." The vet lab tech assistant was properly impressed. "Darned near."

"HOW YOU FEELIN', Wayne?" Doc Crasner teased the steady wrangler back in the pens where the Coggins testing continued Saturday morning.

It was as plain as the nose on his pained face that Wayne was suffering terribly from a hangover. He and the other boys had really tied one on the night before at the Blue Moon, and all of them were sweating profusely in the sunny, rapidly warming New Mexico day. Still, there was the cowboy code and all.

"Doin' fine, Doc," Wayne fibbed through tight teeth. Doc laughed. These cowboys would rather die than let you know they were hurting.

"I'm dyin'." The vet lab tech's assistant groaned. He did not have to live up to the cowboy code and wasn't planning on adopting it any time soon. At least not on this morning after.

"Come on, now, buddy," Wayne teased him. "You didn't drink half as much as the rest of us."

"Oh, don't remind me."

Wayne, Doc, and the vet lab tech all laughed.

"Remind you of what?" Johnny Dupree popped out of nowhere behind Doc Crasner. Cool Daddy was by Johnny's side.

"Booze." The assistant tried to smile.

"You hang in there, man." Johnny grinned.

"Maybe you should have a beer right now," Cool Daddy suggested with a twinkle in his eye.

"Oh." The assistant groaned again. All the cowboys laughed heartily.

"Stick with us." Johnny slapped him on the shoulder. "We'll make a cowboy out of you yet."

"I don't know." The assistant rubbed his aching head.

"Sure we will. You hang with us, you'll see."

The rest of the morning was a repeat of the previous two days of the auction only more of it, lots more of it. Horse trailer after horse trailer streamed in, and the men working behind and in front of the scenes kept up a breakneck speed all through the morning. CB ranged the length and breadth of the area shouting orders, threatening dismissals, cheering good sales, generally keeping a semi-tight rein on the auction overall.

Around twelve thirty, Johnny managed to grab a bite to eat at the snack bar and hustled over to his trailer for a quick, surreptitious beer. He hadn't been inside five minutes when there was a knock at the door. Expecting Luisa back from town, where she had gone apparently to sulk since sometime Friday, or CB there to either fire him or demand that he get back to work immediately, he got an unexpected surprise when he answered the knock.

"Marcie?" It was an odd thing to him to have apparently forgotten he'd spent the night making love to her in her fancy Albuquerque home and had only left her a few hours before. For a moment he just stood at the trailer door looking out at her.

"Well, can I come in?"

"Oh, oh, sure, yeah."

He motioned for her to come in and went back to find his newly opened beer. Before he could get a full swig down, Marcie was on him, grabbing him around the waist, pulling his shirt up, unbuckling his belt.

"Whoa, Nellie." He only vaguely tried to avoid her assault.

In a heartbeat they were in a pile on Johnny's bed, and there was no more reluctance, no turning back. She was wild, just as she had been the night before. Their lovemaking was fast, furious, and not a little on the rough side. It had just ended when there was another knock on the door.

"Oh, crap." Johnny hurriedly pulled his jeans up over his bare skin. "It's CB. He's gonna kick my butt for being late after lunch."

"Who cares? Screw this cowboy job baloney."

"Easy for you to say." He hopped into his boots and pulled on a shirt. "You don't work for CB."

"I wouldn't put up with this kind of demeaning nonsense."

"You would if you wanted to keep a job." He snapped the buttons on his shirt. "That is, if you ever had a job."

"Hmph." Marcie snorted. Johnny opened the door.

"Luisa." He loudly blew out air. "I thought you was CB."

"Can I come in?" Luisa checked out his disheveled appearance.

"Uh, well...."

"I'm coming in." Luisa pushed her way past him.

"Wait."

"Who the hell is *she?"* Luisa saw Marcie in Johnny's bed.

"Who the hell are *you?"* Marcie countered.

"I'll show you who I am, you bitch." Luisa headed straight for the bed. "Messing with my man behind my back."

"Your man?" Marcie huffed, but she grabbed the covers on the bed and pulled back, fearful of Luisa's angry charge. Johnny grabbed Luisa before she could get to Marcie.

"Hold up." He wrapped his arms around Luisa. "Take it easy."

"You bastard." She swung an arm up, which he managed to fend off while still holding her back.

"Calm the hell down."

"You whore," she yelled at Marcie.

"Get your bitch away from me." Marcie jumped out of bed. She cringed against a back wall, naked.

"What did you call me, you rich slut?"

"That's enough." Johnny wrestled Luisa toward the door. "It ain't like we're married or anything. Stop fighting."

"How could you, Johnny?" Luisa began to cry. "With somebody like *her.* I treated you good. You know I did."

"Come on," he cooed to her. "Go on now. I'll talk to you later. Come on."

"You bastard." She sobbed, but her explosive anger was spent. She allowed Johnny to lead her to the door. "After all we meant to each other."

"Go on. I'll see you in a little bit. Up at the auction."

"It's over, Cowboy. You hurt me for the last time. It's over."

"We'll talk later. Go on now."

"You had no right." She let him take her outside. "You had no right. You're a bastard."

"I know, baby, I'm a bastard."

"Not with somebody like her."

"It don't mean nothin'."

"I thought we had something." She pulled away. "But you're like every other man. A cheater and a liar."

"Baby." Johnny checked out the crowded auction grounds. "I gotta get to work."

"Don't expect me to come running back." Luisa walked away. "Never again. You cheatin' bastard."

"That's right. I'm a cheatin' bastard."

"Damn right you are."

"Well, shoot." He turned to go back into his trailer. "Hell's Bells."

SUNDAY NIGHT, AFTER the auction ended, Johnny went home with Marcie. He parked his trailer at a nearby KOA and followed her silver Mercedes back into Albuquerque. She had a big, bright, airy condo down in Old Albuquerque near the Rio Grande. The condo's two expansive levels had shiny hardwood floors, high ceilings, and large windows offering a pleasant view of both the old city out front and the new Albuquerque in back.

The interior was, naturally enough, in southwestern style with lots of Navajo reds and greens and very comfortable chairs and couches. Also, naturally enough, Johnny felt out of place there, off kilter. It was maybe what Marcie was shooting for.

"Are you one of those men who can't deal with a successful, independent woman?" She had grilled Johnny on their fourth day of living under her roof. They had just had sex and were lying in bed together, John under the covers not touching Marcie, she on top, without clothes.

"What?" In the few days he'd been with Marcie he'd already seen flashes of a mercurial, sarcastic, and occasionally vicious side.

"Are you threatened by me? By my money, my condo, my success?"

"Shoot. I don't think I'd actually thought about it."

"I think you have male issues."

"Male issues. What the hell are those?"

"I thought so." She acted as if she had caught him in some huge lie.

"Huh?"

"You don't like it when a woman is free and independent. You want to control her, dominate her."

"Like I just did." He rolled over and pulled her toward him. She squirmed away, covered herself with an edge of the covers.

"Don't touch me."

"Jesus Christ. If that's the way you want it."

"See? See?"

"Holy crap." He got out of bed. "See *what?* I'm getting' out of here for a while. I don't know what's gotten into you."

"Go on, then."

"Hell, I'm going."

He started putting on his pants. She pulled him back to her on the bed.

"Don't go." She was suddenly as hot and welcoming as she had been cold and distant. "Let's do it again."

"Jeez, woman, make up your mind."

"Shut up and do me."

"DO I HAVE male issues?" Johnny sipped on a beer at his sister Kate's kitchen table.

"What the hell are you talking about?" She tried to laugh, but it came out in staccato bursts in between coughs.

"Have you been to the doctor?" Johnny was concerned.

Kate was unusually haggard and tired, even for her and her lifetime of medical hassles. He tried to be a good big brother to her, especially with their dad gone and all, but she was a free-spirited woman, proud and insistent on taking care of herself.

"I'm fine, it's just a cough. Nothing to worry about."

"You sure?"

"I thought we were talking about your male issues."

"Yeah, I guess so."

"Well, what do you think?"

"I don't even know what that means, but it sounds bad somehow." Kate coughed and laughed.

"Are you a man?"

"What kind of a silly…?"

"Well?"

"Of course I am."

"Then there's your answer."

"There's my answer?"

"You're a man. You have male issues."

"Seriously, Kate?"

"You're a cowboy. You're a man. You have male issues by definition."

"Is that bad?"

"I guess to some people."

"What should I do?

"There's nothing to do. You are who you are."

"Well, hell, now I don't get it at all."

Kate came around the table and hugged him from behind.

"You're Cowboy. That's who you are. That's all you need to know."

"I don't know, Kate." He held his sister's hand in his. "I don't know if it is."

ON A COOL evening, late in the week after he had visited Kate, Johnny and Marcie attended a Southwestern art show at a gallery near Marcie's condo. There had been glasses of wine, hors d'oeuvres, lots of high falutin' people, and talk. Johnny had been bored out of his mind and completely, totally out of his element. Back at Marcie's place, the common conflict that had come to define their non-sexual relationship immediately flared up.

"You hated it, didn't you?" Marcie wanted to know as soon as they had put up their coats. Johnny headed for the refrigerator for a cold bottle of beer.

"Hated what?" He dug past package after package of foods he didn't recognize to extract a beer from the back of the ice box.

"You know very well what I mean."

Johnny opened the beer, turned, and walked back out into the living room where Marcie stood before a black-and-white striped love seat that always made him think of a cow.

"Nope, ain't got a clue."

"You're intimidated by my friends, by my crowd."

"Bored, maybe." He took a deep drink of beer and let out a loud belch. Marcie rolled her eyes.

"It's the same thing from day one. You can't deal with my success, my independence."

"Maybe I should go?"

"Running from change. The exact opposite of what Doctor Tucker recommended."

"Who?"

"Doctor Tucker. You met him tonight at the gallery."

"The little bald-headed guy with that harpy of a wife?" He plopped down in a big chair across from the loveseat. "You talked to him about me, us?"

"She's very *avant-garde,* and he's the best psychologist in Albuquerque. He said you had very old-fashioned ideas about women. You should go see him. I could make you an appointment."

"I don't think so."

"You need counseling. You're way too macho with women. You think we're just sexual objects."

"Damn it. You sound like you're one of those women who can't tell the difference between one guy and all the others."

"You're very defensive. Did you know that? Combative and hostile. Do you know why?"

"No, I don't, but I bet you're going—"

The ringing of Marcie's phone cut him off. He was actually glad that it did. This conversation, like several others they had recently had, was going nowhere. She might be good in bed, but she was a real pain out of it.

"It's for you." She acted like the call was some kind of affront to her.

He stood up slow, walked over, and took the phone from her. She watched him, listened to his end of the conversation, heard his happy tone at first, then the concern creep into his voice, finally a monotone response as if he had lost all interest in what was being said. He hung up the phone, turned toward her with a vacant look in his eyes.

"Kate," he managed to say, his voice a dull, lifeless projection.

"Oh, what now?" Marcie acted annoyed. "What's she complaining about this time? You know you treat her like a little baby. Sometimes I think you love her more than me. Your relationship is a little odd if you ask me. I think you should...."

But her final judgements were lost on Johnny. He had walked right out the door of the condo and shut it behind him without uttering another word. When she reached the door and looked out after him, he was long gone.

FOR THREE DAYS after tracking Johnny down and calling him at the new girlfriend's house, Buddy Harris was still looking for his old friend. Kate's sudden, unexpected death had caught them all off guard, and it had taken some time to locate Johnny at the new woman's place. And Buddy could tell from his voice that the bad news had devastated him. Worse yet, he had then just hung up and disappeared.

Buddy tried to find him first by checking with all the guys from the auction, but no one had seen him. Then he tried all their familiar haunts. The Blue Moon bar, a couple of restaurants in Los Lunas, a ranch northwest of Albuquerque where he and Johnny had helped with a roundup the previous year. But no luck.

He called the girlfriend again, but she was so snotty Buddy just hung up on her and went on with the search by himself. Finally, it occurred to him that Johnny might be at a KOA where he sometimes parked his trailer when he was out of work or out of town or just wanted to drive his pickup.

KATE'S DEATH KILLED something inside Johnny Dupree. He was now totally alone, like a child orphan. No father, no sister. No one. He felt as unsure of himself as if the ground upon which he walked were nothing more than sinking, shifting sand. He felt dead to the world.

He didn't cry. And he didn't feel. He tried to feel. He drank countless beers in search of feeling, but there was nothing there. The drunker he got the further from feeling he became. It was no use. Nothing could make it right. Nothing could make him feel or feel better. In a stupor he called Marcie.

"If I'd been there," he slurred over the phone, "she might not have died. I wasn't there for her."

"I doubt," Marcie's tone was cold as ice, *"that you have ever been there for any woman."*

When she started up on the "male issues" talk again, he had the sense to hang up. But his life was nothing but confusion to him now. It had turned so quickly. He couldn't remember anymore that he had been a horseman, a cowboy.

His life on the ranches and at the arenas and auctions faded into a hazy background, mixed up with memories of his dead father and sister. They had been all he really had. Now they were gone. Both of them. He was completely alone in the world. Confused and vulnerable, the very states of being that Marcie had seen in him and attacked.

To forget, he continued to drink. To drink all the time. But it did not help. He could not feel or forget or resolve. Finally, in a brief moment of perceived lucidity, a plan occurred to him. He set out immediately to complete it. He got into his pickup and headed for Kate's apartment, seeing the world coldly, in the narrow fog created by too much drink and too much thought and too much suppressed or lost feeling.

JOHNNY WAS NOT at the KOA when Buddy finally got to it, but he had been. The trailer was full of beer cans and dirty clothes. There was no sign of him. He checked with the owners, but they didn't remember seeing Johnny there or his pickup. After thinking the situation over, Buddy guessed there could be only one other possible place to look.

Walking up the sidewalk to Kate's apartment, Buddy felt the hair stand up on the back of his neck. He was grieving Kate's death, too, he'd known her almost all her life, but there was something else wrong. He could feel it.

The door to her apartment was unlocked. That didn't seem right. And it wasn't. He hurried into the apartment, calling out Johnny's name. There was no sign of him in the living or dining room or the hall bathroom.

He found him in the back bedroom of the apartment.

"Damn it, Johnny!" he cried out when he had to look up at the ceiling fan and overhead light to find his friend, the friend he had known for so many of the key years in each of their young lives. "Damn it to hell."

BUDDY TOLD ALL the wranglers and cowboys from out at Charles Beltre's auction barn about Johnny, but after just telling one, the news was all over Los Lunas, and the story even made some of the local papers. Everybody knew about it within days. Most of the auction crew was at his funeral, as was Luisa—crying and in black—but nobody saw the fancy woman from Albuquerque.

The boys all got together that night at the Blue Moon to drink too much beer and tell funny and poignant stories about Johnny "Cowboy." Then, like it always does, life went on for the living, soon returning to its normal rhythms, but without the person who passed—without his passions, his laughter, his issues, his humanity.

In the fall after Johnny's death, Charles Beltre put on another horse auction out at his Los Lunas auction barn. All the usual crew was there—Pancho, Buddy, Cool Daddy, Givers, Wayne, Judy climbing up onto the pen fences to show off her feminine wares, and of course CB himself, the guided missile—swearing, yelling, acting like he wasn't making money hand over fist.

On Saturday of the auction, Buddy was standing outside the snack bar on the west side of the barn with Luisa when they saw Marcie drive by in a silver Mercedes. Luisa couldn't contain a curse.

"There's that bitch, the one that ruined Cowboy."

"Yeah, I see her."

"She's got some nerve, coming around here after what she did."

"Ain't no tellin' what caused Cowboy to do it."

"I know." Luisa was certain in her conviction. "It was that bitch."

"Well, it don't matter now, anyhow. He's gone."

Their heads down, he and Luisa turned to walk back into the barn. Marcie drove on past, at least appearing to not notice either of them. She drove her Mercedes on out to the stop sign at the T-intersection with the blacktop road running east and west beyond the auction grounds. After a brief pause, she made a right and headed back toward the interstate, on back to Albuquerque.

In the barn arena, things went on as usual. Pancho was showing a Bay mare, CB was complaining about anything and everything he could, the auctioneer's rapid-fire voice filled the barn while his ring men worked the bidders, the wranglers helped the vet with the Coggins testing, and Buddy and a couple of others began rounding up the next horses to be shown. It was a bright and sunny day, a day like any other.

J.B. HOGAN is an award-winning author with some 350 stories and poems and twelve books published. Among his books are *Bar Harbor, Mexican Skies, Time and Time Again, Living Behind Time,* and *Losing Cotton.* He has a Ph.D. in English Literature, worked for many years as a technical writer, and has researched and written extensively on local history. His book *Angels in the Ozarks* is a history of 1930s professional baseball in the area. He helped write *An Illustrated History of the Fayetteville Square* with noted local historian Anthony J. Wappel. His newest local history book, the award-winning *Forgotten Fayetteville and Washington County,* was published in September 2023.

www.ingramcontent.com/pod-product-compliance
Lightning Source LLC
Chambersburg PA
CBHW020910180626
46816CB00007BA/2328

* 9 7 8 1 6 3 3 7 3 9 4 1 3 *